Desperate House Wines

A Full-Bodied Collection of Sinister Short Stories

Marilyn Todd

White City

Press

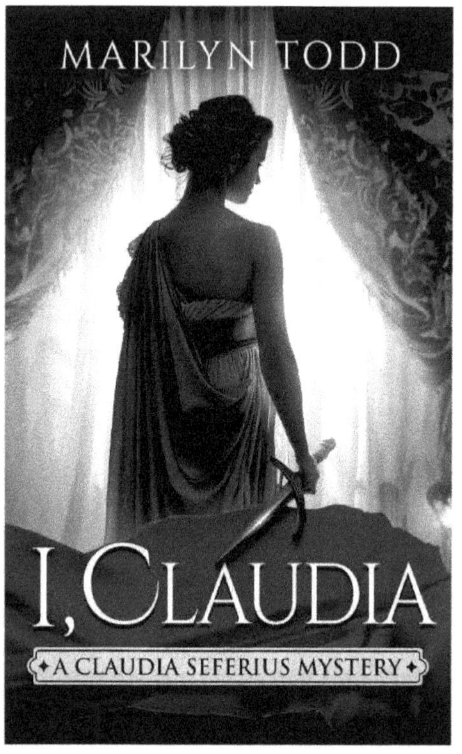

First in the Claudia Seferius mystery series

Set in 13 B. C.

Claudia Seferius has successfully flattered her way into marriage with a wealthy Roman wine merchant. But when her secret gambling debts spiral, she hits on another resourceful way to make money – offering her "personal services" to high-ranking Roman Citizens.

Unfortunately, her clients are now turning up dead – the victims of a sadisitc serial killer.

When Marcus Cornelius Orbilio, the handsome investigating officer, starts digging deep for clues, Claudia realizes she must track down the murderer herself – before her husband discovers what she's been up to.

Paperback ISBN: 9781963479324
eBook ISBN: 9781963479294

Available from https://whitecitypress.com/product/i-claudia/

Desperate House Wines
A Full-Bodied Collection of Sinister Short Stories

Marilyn Todd

Published by White City Press
An imprint of Misti Media LLC
https://whitecitypress.com
Available in both Paperback and eBook Editions
1 2 3 4 5 6 7 8 9 10
Copyright © Marilyn Todd 2025
Paperback ISBN: 9781963479683
eBook ISBN: 9781963479669

The following works have previously appeared in:

Bad Day on Mount Olympus—Mammoth Book of Comic Fantasy
Reprinted by Crippen & Landru

Beach Men—Ellery Queen's Mystery Magazine Feb 2016

Bench Mark—Ellery Queen's Mystery Magazine March/April 2018

Beyond the Tree Line—Ellery Queen's Mystery Magazine May/June 2020

Cover Them with Flowers—Ellery Queen's Mystery Magazine
Reprinted by Crippen & Landru

Death at Delphi—Ellery Queen's Mystery Magazine
Reprinted by Crippen & Landru

Desperate House Wines—Ellery Queen's Mystery Magazine July/Aug 2022

Drawn to Murder—Vautrin 2020

First Dates Are Always Tricky—Ellery Queen's Mystery Magazine Sept/Oct 2018

Leap of Faith—Ellery Queen's Mystery Magazine Aug/Sept 2021

Nights in White Satin—Ellery Queen's Mystery Magazine Jan/Feb 2020

Stage Struck—Ellery Queen's Mystery Magazine 2005

For my lovely friend, Trish,
who knows all about house wines.
And desperate!

Contents

Introduction

You can hide the evidence and bury the body –but you can't bury the truth or hide from retribution.

From theft to murder via double cross, they all think they're smarter than justice.

Whether they choose poison, arson, bullets or rope, will they get away with their crime?

Bad Day on Mount Olympus

The meeting was going well. Boring, but hey. They only come round once a year. Who's going to quibble about the odd satyr too fond of his own voice to relinquish the floor? Or some nerd of a faun who's all presentation-this, flip-chart-that? Let it ride, that's what I say. If these guys get off on pie-charts and graphs, who am I to begrudge them their fun? Not everyone's idea of a good time is freeflowing wine and the chance to get to know one another afterwards.

By which, of course, I mean sex.

And lots of it.

Also, you get to catch up with the gossip. After all, Cupid's still a kid. Not every shot is on target. Some really interesting alliances can result. *Plus*—a real bonus, this—we get to see who's been turned into what animal, tree, bug or whatever. Naturally, this year's big story was Io. *Apparently* (and this you didn't get this from me), but *apparently* Juno walked in on Jupiter relieving Io of the rather cumbersome burden of her virginity and…

Look. Let's just say the wife wasn't any too pleased at the picture, OK?

Well, we all know what a bitch Juno can be when she's mad. Look what she did to me. I'm her friend. Anyhow, Jupiter's thinking he'd best get in first, if he's looking to protect the girlfriend, so… Spotting a herd of cows on the hill, quick as a flash, he turns Io into a heifer. Find her among *that* lot, he smarms to the wife. But this was the thing, see. Juno didn't *want* to go looking for Io. 'Who needs it?' she says. 'Didn't I always say she was a scheming little cow?' (Incidentally, Io's apologies for absence at this AGM have been duly noted.)

Anyways, like I said, the meeting's going well. After a few millennia you get to know the pattern and this was the point on the schedule when whichever river god was spouting off this time would begin to run out of steam. Happens every year. Someone, somewhere, gets fed up with what he's doing and wastes hours of precious drinking time by making out a lengthy case for changing course. The response from the rest of us is the same each year, too. We let the old windbag make his speech and then say yes. The reason we don't say yes straight off is that then some other windbag would get up and start making demands. So we let it run and then pretend to vote according to our conscience. Of course, the reason we *all* say yes *every* time is that if we didn't, we'd lose even *more* drinking time during the debate. This is democracy, see. It's the only way to do business.

So we vote. The motion's carried. Some little stream in Arcadia (or was it Thrace?) will change course and the river god, bless his sediment, duly gets his change of scenery. Tedious or wot? But any minute now Sagittarius, half-man, half-horse who's chaired the last three hundred meetings, will start to wind things up. We'll get the usual jeers of Sagittarius always wanting to be the "centaur of attention". Some wag will ask Pan, doesn't *he* want to, ho ho, "pipe up" with a question. And someone else will accuse Orpheus of "lute behaviour" in a public place. The usual stuff. Old as Olympus. And call us sad, but we still find it funny.

By the time our equine chairman was rolling up his scrolls and murmuring 'Any other business?' Bacchus is already on his cloven feet, heading for the wine. We almost missed the voice boom out 'Yes' from the back…

Yes? You could have blown me down with a feather. (Well, you could have, if I'd had a body to blow down).

'Er.' Sagittarius stamped a hoof, whinnied a bit, and you can see what was going through his head. Nothing like this had ever happened before on Mount Olympus. 'Did someone say yes?'

See, after him asking 'Any other business', there's always the same short silence, when everyone *pretends* they're trying to think up a question (most of us being more polite than Bacchus). Then we shake our heads, like how we'd all have *loved* to raise a point or three but since the meeting covered everything on *our* agenda, boy, were we stumped. At this point, when Sagittarius pronounces the AGM closed, a cheer goes up loud enough to cause a landslip in Crete followed by a stampede to the wine. Hey! It's not called the "Amorous Gluttonous Massing" for nothing, you know.

Except now someone was spoiling the fun.

'Me,' the voice said. 'I have a point I'd like to raise.'

Necks craned for a better view. Who was this party pooper, we all demanded. And couldn't someone tear his damned head off or something?

The reason we couldn't see him was that, until now, he'd been sitting down. Wise move. Had we noticed him beforehand, we'd all have guessed he'd be trouble and taken the necessary counter measures to keep him quiet. Like sit on him or something. Because no-one wears the full lion's pelt on a sweltering hot day like this without courting *some* kind of disaster.

'Ah. Hercules.'

I don't *believe* it! Sagittarius, the knucklehead, was inviting him up to the front. At the same time, I noticed a lot of eyes turn longingly at the wine jugs. Not least Bacchus's. Although, in fairness, I have to say most of Hundred-Eyed Argus's gaze was directed straight down the bosom of that little wood sprite from Corinth.

Swinging his olivewood club as though it weighed no more than a sunbeam, our doughty hero stepped onto the stage. 'Mister Chairman,' he drawled, flexing his pecs. 'Fauns, satyrs, nymphs, dryads, maenads—'

'Gonads!' yelled a heckler from the crowd, and you can see where *his* thoughts were headed. OK, so we all know that sex isn't everything. But come on. There's more than enough hanging around in between as it is.

'—and all my fellow Immortals.' It was satisfying to watch the sweat pour down Hercules' face under the heavy lion's head. Not so good that he produced a thick wad of notes from somewhere deep in its pelt. 'For some considerable time,' he read, 'there has been an awareness among each and every one of us that all is not well on Mount Olympus. Morale has never been lower—'

How swiftly the mood of the crowd changed! With each bass syllable which carried across the clearing in the woods, they forgot about the wine, the partying, the reason they came here in the first place. Ears pricked up. Backs straightened. Lips pursed in concentration. At last they were not forced to endure some nebulous whinge, a trivial piece of planning which needed approval, an excuse for self-congratulation and praise. This speech embraced them all. *Their* needs. *Their* hopes. *Their* ambitions, *their* prospects. A breathless silence descended as Hercules proceeded to outline the riches he felt the Immortals deserved. What rewards they should reap.

Page after page turned in the big man's hand until, having raised them right up, having lifted the crowd to the very summit of spiritual aspiration, cleverly he began to trawl through their grievances. He listed the niggles which had eroded their confidence over the years. The petty bureaucracies imposed by the gods which stood in their way. I felt, rather than heard, the rumble which surged through the clearing. An emotion pitched somewhere between approval, fear and excitement...

Couldn't they see what he was planning? *Didn't they care?* With each fervoured agreement, each enthusiastic nod of the head, each vociferous 'hear, hear!' which fell louder and louder from their lips I myself grew that much colder.

'So I put it to you, brothers, that the gods—those men and women who laughingly refer to themselves as our masters—have not only grown lack-lustre and idle, they have become spiteful and careless, abusing their powers. Moreover, brothers....' Hercules paused. 'These presumed masters, these so-called invincible beings, have not only lost interest in the running of mortal affairs on earth, I say they have proved themselves *incompetent* here on Olympus.'

Oh, shit. There it was, out in the open. An overthrow. A coup. A take-over. Revolution.

'Incompetent,' he repeated forcefully.

You can say it six times over, *brother,* but this is not for me. I am out of here…

'By way of example, take little Echo here.'

'Here!' I protested. Oh, I do *so* not want any part of this—

'Look at the spiteful way Juno punished that poor little nymph.'

Well, that bit was true. Juno's revenge *had* been harsh. But hell, I knew the risks when I took them, keeping her talking time and again while Jupiter made his getaway from whichever pretty young thing he'd been seducing. I knew full well what would happen if she ever found out. She'd deprive me the power of speech—and for ever. Only Jupiter's intervention left me with some kind of voice. The gift, if that's what it is, of repetition.

'Not once did Juno punish the poor creature,' Hercules said, 'but little Echo was made to suffer twice over. What a bitch! What a spiteful, malicious bitch. And this, brothers, is supposed to be justice under the rule of the Queen of Olympus, the one and only Mighty Juno!'

'No!' I cried out.

Not true. Juno played no part in my doomed love for Narcissus. But, alas, no-one could hear me…

'Not content with robbing Echo of her voice,' our muscled hero was saying, 'she takes the poor kid's body away, too.'

'Ooh,' I protested.

Unfair. Hercules knows damned well I pined away out of love. That was my choice, my decision. You can't pin that one on Juno. If I could not belong to Narcissus, I would not belong to anyone else. And I tell you something else, *brother.* I've never regretted that. Not for an instant. But Hercules had his audience right where he wanted them. Which meant he wouldn't let a little thing like the truth get in the way…

'When Juno saw Narcissus waiting for Echo at the pool, she couldn't resist adding insult to injury. She made him fall in love with himself.'

'Sylph,' I corrected firmly.

No-one but me and Narcissus knows what happened down there by that pool. Being dormant right now, Narcissus can't tell and I sure as hell won't. Some things are personal. But I won't have it bandied around that Narcissus fell in love with his own reflection. That just wasn't true. And frankly it bothers me that if Hercules goes on repeating that rumour, that's how it will end up being believed.

Look how he was playing them now! Not a dry eye in the clearing, and that included Hundred-Eyed Argus. Hell, I know everyone's a sucker for that somebody-done-somebody-wrong shit. I just didn't approve of Hercules using *me* to win his audience over. To show them that the deities on Olympus weren't as intelligent or as resourceful as they'd have us believe.

And now he was about to muscle in and oust them, with the backing of this gullible band! I looked round at my comrades. Woodnymphs and fauns, gorgons and sirens, cyclops, titans and sibyls. Over there, Arachne, turned by Pallas into a spider for no better reason than having woven a better tapestry than the goddess. Lycaon, changed into a snarling, howling wolf for doubting Jupiter. Midas, given the ears of an ass for siding with Pan against Apollo. Atalanta turned into a lioness by Venus just (would you believe!) for consummating her marriage, poor cow.

Up they surfaced, though. Grudges which had festered over the centuries. Rancour which had grown bitter with each passing millennium. Centaurs, bacchants, fountain nymphs, muses, harpies, furies, those unfortunate men and women turned into stone all began to dredge up their resentment. For most, though, the prospect of power was simply too tantalising to resist...

'No more tyrants!' Hercules cried, thumping his fist into the palm of his hand.

'No more tyrants!' came the rallying chorus.

'Democracy for Olympus!' he roared.

'Democracy for Olympus!' they cried, and I thought, yeah. Io isn't the only one stuck in a herd.

'In place of Jupiter and Juno,' Hercules said, 'I propose a triumvirate.'

Took him long enough to get round to it, eh? The tyrant is dead, long live the tyrant. But the baying mob cheered him on.

'Are you with me?' he urged. *'Are you with me?'*

Back came the predictable roar, the applause, the tumultuous stamp of approval.

'Then I propose three men at its head—myself, and the heroic twins. What do you say, Immortals? What do you say to democracy led by Hercules, Castor and Pollux?'

I knew what I had to say.

'Pollux!' I said. And I sighed. Dammit, *someone* had to put paid to this midsummer madness.

I just wished that someone didn't have to be me…

* * *

Don't get me wrong. I'm no fan of the gods, I don't fawn and flatter them like some I could mention. Well, all right. Who I *will* mention. Ganymede, for one, the oily little oik. OK, so he was a shepherd boy plucked from obscurity to become cup-bearer to the gods, but does he really have to suck up to them in the repulsive way that he does? Then there's Janus. He's not two-faced for nothing, you know—

But you're right. This is not the time to start bitching. We'll go into that later, once we've got this revolt bedded down. The problem was, of course, *how* to stop Hercules from toppling Jupiter from his throne.

Now it's not as though I personally believe the gods are infallible. Hercules made many valid points and I'd be the first to admit there's ample room for improvement. The Olympians *have* grown indolent. Mistakes *have* been made. They've become careless, underhanded, ethics have gone out the window and if ever there was a time to wheel out the clichés this was it. Power corrupts, blah, blah, blah. But! And this is the thing. *The same would be true if Hercules and the twins took control.*

Within no time they, too, would become self-serving tyrants, who would notice the difference? Find me an altruistic politician and I'll show you glaciers on the equator. Oh, and cut the crap about doing it for the Good Of The People. Hercules performed twelve Labours all right, and magnificently so I might add. But they were not for the Good Of The People. He mucked out stables and slew lions and hydras and wot-have-you for his own ends, remember. That this son of a mortal might himself become a god.

And you can forget Castor and Pollux. One's a wrestler, the other's a boxer—sporting heroes without doubt. But have you spotted a single brain cell between them? Keep looking! No, in Hercules' book these brawnballs were nothing more than walking, talking advertising hoardings. "You are safe in our hands" was the message. The Immortals flocked to their feet.

So what was *my* problem, you ask? If one order is the same as another, why not go with the flow? We-ell. Ask yourself this. Would you want *your* destiny in the hands of a group of drunken revellers who yawn their way through their own AGM and who change sides at the first bit of oratory? I rest my case.

The problem was, where to start. Jupiter was off on one of his wenching sprees, and who knows what disguise he'd adopted this time. Swans, showers of gold, husband impersonations, there was no telling – and certainly not enough time to find out. Hercules wasn't stupid. He knew full well he was carrying the Immortals along on the tide. He intended to strike before they changed their minds. So who did that leave? Neptune? Uh-uh. Too busy whipping up storms and sinking the ships of some little Greek island he felt had neglected him. Apollo? Still driving his fiery chariot across the skies over our heads. As for Mars, well damn me, hadn't he turned himself into a ruddy bull again? (After Io, I'll bet!)

This, then, looked like being a job for the girls.

* * *

After a hard day's chase through the forests or a bit of post-prandial nookie, there's really nothing quite like unwinding over a good gossip with friends. OK, so I use the term loosely. Maybe the girls meet up more for the mutual massaging of egos than friendship, but who cares? On this particular occasion I hit lucky. It was the A-Team splashing about under the waterfall.

Diana, needing the usual reassurance that she was the swiftest. Venus, bragging about Adonis, so everyone knew she was the fairest. Minerva, head in a book. (Like we didn't know she was the brainy one!) Plus, of course, Juno, angling for sympathy now that everyone knew Jupiter was out playing eeny-meeny-maenad-mo again.

Diana was practising her javelin stance in the water's reflection. 'Where's Cupid today?' she was asking his mother.

'That little pest!' You could never accuse Venus of suffocating Cupid with maternal instincts. 'I sent him off to practise in the butts.'

An order, believe me, which Cupid takes literally. And it's bloody painful, I tell you, when that arrow hits home. I heard Adonis couldn't sit down for a week and Vulcan says his scar *still* won't heal.

'I don't know what he sees in these mortal women,' Juno was saying. 'Strumpets, the lot of them.'

'Ahem,' I said. It invariably takes an age to catch someone's attention. You have to wait for just the right moment.

Bugger. This wasn't it.

'Well, you know what they say about husbands, darling,' laughed Venus. 'They're like fires. They go out if you neglect them.'

'Ahem!'

'Are you suggesting I'm not stoking Jupiter's passions, you bitch?'

Oh-oh. This wasn't going the way I had hoped. They were too busy starting a catfight to listen to echoes round the edge of the pool. Briefly, listening to the squabble break out, I was tempted to call it a day. Let Hercules *lead* his raggletaggle band to glory.

I slipped away at the point where Venus was offering to give Juno lessons in techniques of the bedchamber. I was willing to bet that, at this rate, the next time I saw Venus, she'd have her fringe combed over one eye to hide the shiner.

What to do, what to do…

Back in the clearing the Immortals were drunk with both power and wine. Not so much ambrosia and nectar for them, I thought. More like lotus eaters. One taste and everything else is forgotten. I looked at them. Sons and daughters of mortal women rising up against their own parents. Even Hercules, son of Jupiter and fostered by Juno at one stage, was prepared to overthrow his own father and that, I thought, told the story. That was what separated men from the gods.

Olympians might throw tantrums.

Mortal men yearn only for violence.

That's why Hercules would never be King of the Gods. OK, Jupiter has his faults. Serial adultery by no means the least. But was Hercules – indeed were any one of the rabble massed in the clearing – genuinely interested in the welfare of ordinary people? Did they see them as anything other than pawns in their own selfish power game?

Back at the pool, Juno and Venus had joined forces to turn on Diana.

'You can shut your trap,' Juno was saying. 'The day I take advice from virgins about sex is the day my husband turns celibate.'

'How dare you!' Diana snarled. 'I value my virginity—'

'Rubbish,' Venus sneered back. 'No man will have you, you prissy little cow. That's why, after all these millennia, you're still a virgin. You're frigid.'

'Frigid?'

Diana's spluttering drowned the splash of the waterfall and, since it was turning into a right old scrum over there, I left the three of them to it. It was Minerva I focussed on. You notice she hadn't uttered a squeak about Jupiter's philanderings or Diana's chastity bent? (Told you she was the brainy one). I waited until she came to the end of the scroll she was reading – or at least pretending to read, take your pick. Because I know which I'd have sooner been watching, kiddo. Three top goddesses at it hammer and tongs or a dull old page of poetry? No contest. Anyway, as Minerva reached down, I gave the signal.

With a groan that cut through to the marrow, my old friend Boreas, the north wind, spread out his feathers, beat his grey wings and scattered Minerva's scrolls to all points of the compass.

Everyone shivered at the unexpected drop in temperature. Even me. It had been ages since I'd dallied with Boreas, I'd forgotten how icy his embrace could be. But Boreas whipping up Minerva's papers was the signal for Daphne to start. The distinctive rustle of her leathery leaves echoed round the wooded glade, a cue for Myrrh to begin weeping thick, sticky ooze from her bark. Suddenly, all my other friends descended. Ceyx and Alcyone, whose wish to become seabirds had been granted, swooped out of nowhere. Snakes rustled among the long grasses. All those gentle creatures who had asked—yes, *asked!*—to be changed from human shape descended now round the pool, calling at the tops of their voices as Boreas kicked up a din of his own.

'What the hell's up?' Juno was forced to shout over the racket of birdsong and animal sounds and the wild woodland echoes.

'Up!' I yelled back.

'It's that bloody AGM,' Diana snapped, rubbing the goosepimples on her arm. 'Happens every time we leave them alone. Something always goes awry.'

'Wry,' I said, fixing hard on Minerva.

'What the blazes does Apollo think he's playing at up there?' Venus said, glancing up at the sun, still blazing brightly in its innocence. 'I'm bloody freezing.'

'*Zing!*'

'Did you hear that?' Juno sniffed. 'Even scatty little Echo has got in on the act.'

Ooh, you don't know how much I wished she'd said something that I could have replied to at that!

'Sssh,' said Minerva, and the other three goddesses swung round on her, ready to lay into Jupiter's favourite daughter. (You notice how quickly they change sides, these girls. Loyalty changes hands faster than coins in a pickpocket gang).

'Don't tell *me* to shut up, you bossy cow—'

'No, listen,' Minerva said, and there was a tone to her voice that made everyone shut up, not just the three squabbling beauties. The glade plunged into silence. Even the tears of the cataract seemed to fall softly. The laurel stopped shivering. The bird calls ceased. The serpents stopped writhing. Only Myrrh's resin continued to weep.

'All of you, listen to Echo,' Minerva ordered.

Oh, bless you, Minerva. You're not the Goddess of Wisdom for nothing! I let my repetitions echo into the still summer air.

'Up,' I repeated. 'Wry. Zing.'

'Do you hear that?' Minerva reached for her armour.

'Up. Wry. Zing,' I said, softly now. Hurry up, ladies. I was running out of zing here myself.

'By the heavens!' Diana thundered, strapping her quiver on to her back. 'We hear you, Echo. By all the gods, we hear what you're telling us. Trust me, you'll find the Olympians grateful!'

No-one ever accused Juno of being quick on the uptake, but finally the bronze penny dropped.

'*UPRISING?*'

Oh-oh. I recognised *that* tone from the Queen of Olympus.

Someone, somewhere was going to pay.

For once, I was thankful that that someone wouldn't be me!

* * *

I won't bore you with the details. No coup is bloodless, and suffice to say there are a lot of wild bears and boars and snakes running about who'd far rather have remained river gods, satyrs and fauns. Especially now the hunting season's nearly upon us.

But there you go.

For my part, I'm pleased with the outcome. One day, perhaps, men *will* take over from the gods and that will be a sad day for mortals. It is the nature of men to always want to war with one another—and who will be there to quench the fires of hatred, if not Jupiter, Juno, Minerva, et al?

My only regret was that Hercules was taken out of circulation before he could retract his scurrilous lies about me and Narcissus, but what the hell? My lover and I might be condemned to false history, but the truth of our love shows itself every spring. And don't tell *me* some bloke called Wordsworth or Jobsworth or whatever won't want to write a poem in the future about the fruits of our ardour!

As for Hercules, he and the twins didn't disappear entirely. Being a son of Jupiter, his Twelve Labours were given a positive spin in the history books, while at the same time any mention of this little episode was duly deleted. Ditto Castor and Pollux. The gods, being gods, wouldn't kill them, of course. That's not in their nature. So, if you care to tilt your head upwards on a clear night you can see them. Up there in the heavens.

Only you and I know the real reason the three of them have been placed in the Constellation.

And I, of course, am not telling.

At least. Not unless you top up my glass…

Beach Men

These are dangerous waters.

Looking at them now, calm seas, blue sky, just a gentle breeze tickling the grass in the dunes, you don't see the treachery.

But it's there.

A network of ever-changing channels and sandbanks that have claimed thousands of lives over the years, from sailors to fishermen to the men who died trying to rescue them from the ships that foundered here.

Unquestionably the most dangerous waters around Britain.

'Are you sure I can't bring you anything, Harriet? Tea? Water? Something a little stronger, perhaps?'

'Thank you, Father, but no.'

Was my voice shaking? I hoped not. My hands were a tad clammy a few hours earlier. But not now. Not any longer.

I closed my eyes, picturing the wide, sweeping beaches that went on for ever. Heard the sound of the gulls in my head. The slap of waves on the shore.

It wasn't always that calm. Fifty years ago, just a few miles up the coast, *HMS Invincible,* on her way to attack the Danish fleet, ran aground and was torn to shreds by the wind, with a loss of four hundred lives. Six years later, here at Caister, one hundred and forty-four bodies washed ashore after a gale. And three decades after that, the Great Storm of 1836 stranded no fewer than twenty-three vessels.

Dangerous, dangerous waters.

Treacherous, treacherous sandbanks.

A sea monster, that sucked up ships and spat out the bones of the dead.

'Fifteen minutes, Harriet. Are you sure—?'

'Quite sure, Father. And please. If you could just leave me alone…?'

'Of course.' His smile was tight. 'If that's what you want.'

'It is.'

This time I knew my voice was firm and unwavering, and when the door closed, I heaved a sigh of relief. I didn't want him. I didn't want people. I just needed to be alone with my thoughts.

My thoughts were all I had left.

* * *

And those thoughts led me, inevitably, to the Watch Tower. A tall, seemingly impossible wooden structure perched on top of a (dare I say it?) pole that the local people erected, in an attempt to put an end to the carnage. Manned in bad weather by the beach men of Caister, from this vantage point they could see at once when the sandbanks claimed another victim.

And off they would set! In howling gales and monstrous high seas, while thunder crashed and lightning crackled, to rescue the poor souls held in the jaws of the monster.

Brave, brave men.

Risking their lives in the smallest of vessels. Some in tiny rowing boats, some in fishing boats. Ketches or yawls, I can't tell the difference—something to do with the sails, I believe, but I am a city girl. From London. The countryside is as alien to me as these wild, majestic, windswept beaches that hide the dark nature of the beast.

The dark nature that hides inside us all.

* * *

'Ten minutes, Harriet.'

Go away, I wanted to scream.

'Thank you,' I said. How polite was that?

But inside, I could still hear the screaming. Of winds, screeching wilder than banshees. Of men, trapped by fallen masts, mangled in the rigging, crushed between the timbers. For hours we clung to the wreckage, while the storm raged around us and the monster mangled its prey. Until finally, through the blackness, we saw lights bobbing towards us over the waters. Heard shouts. The sweet cries of deliverance.

'Women and children first!'

No children on board. In fact, I was the only female. Drenched to the skin, cold to the marrow, and my teeth chattering like castanets out of control, I climbed into the boat and saw my dress dripped with the blood of dead and dying sailors.

But salvage comes with a price.

Sometimes, the captains of the stricken vessels might negotiate terms with the beach men. Sometimes, conditions were so dire that it was just a question of recovering whatever goods the beach men could find. They believed the system was fair. Ships foundered, even in the worst storms, for one of three reasons. Poor navigation, poor maintenance, or poor crew. Because they took payment, the beach men were called looters, pirates, mercenaries, thieves.

But only by people whose lives hadn't been saved.

'Five minutes, Harriet. That's all, I'm afraid.'

Ah, but five minutes was more than enough. You see, the ship carrying me was a sturdy little collier that had been delivering coal—so valuable it was known as black diamonds—to London. On its return trip, it was taking me to a new life in Newcastle-upon-Tyne, as well as sand that served as ballast on the voyage, but which was also an essential component for the sizeable glass making industry on Tyneside.

Ballast? Not exactly rich pickings for the poor souls who'd risked their lives, limbs and livelihoods in a violent storm.

Which is how the captain came to invite the beach men to help themselves to whatever they could find.

How they came to heave my trunk ashore.

And find the body of my husband curled up inside, where I'd planned to throw him overboard with the help of my lover.

'I'm sorry, Harriet, but it's time.'

Time indeed. The hangman was waiting. This would be my last walk.

I looked at the pasty-faced priest. Felt no shame as my hands were tied.

My defence that it was suicide cut no ice with the police. Partly because the was knife still in his back, mostly because my lover sang like the proverbial linnet, but like I said. I'm a London girl. The East End, to be precise. Why shouldn't I marry a rich man when offered the chance, then ease him out of the way? I wasn't greedy. I'd booked a passage in his name on a ship bound for the Colonies. Was quite prepared to wait out the seven years before he could be classified dead.

Bloody beach men.

Bench Mark

'Happy birthday, Marcus.'

Orbilio's eyelids couldn't have sprung apart any faster if she'd jabbed him with her brooch pin. Must remember that next time.

'Claudia?'

And who imagined eyes could bulge that wide?

'Wonderful things, the anniversaries of our birth.' She shook out the creases the journey across town had left in her turquoise blue stola, and made a second mental note. Have her steward change the cushions in her litter. Those things this morning were stuffed with dagger blades, lizard bones and a bunch of broken roof tiles. 'The perfect opportunity to take stock of our life. Accept there's no point in dwelling on the past, we can't change it. No point in dwelling on the future, because, despite what those charlatans mutter in the Forum, we can't predict it. Oh, and there's no point in dwelling on the present, either. I haven't brought you one.'

He struggled to prop himself up on one elbow without disturbing the bulge snuggled next to him beneath his fine damascene coverlet, its ribcage rising and falling in sleep. 'I'm not even going to ask how you got past the guard dog, the janitor, a household of loyal servants as well as my poor beleaguered manservant.' Funny how quickly surprise can turn into suspicion 'But I would like to know what you're doing in my bedroom.'

'Not the same as her, I can assure you.' Claudia gave the bulge a kick and was rewarded with a satisfying growl. 'Now do come along, Orbilio, I have something to show you and it's urgent—*Janus!*' She sprang back. *'What in Hades is THAT?'*

'A wolfhound.' He grinned. 'Big buggers, aren't they?'

'I've seen dray horses half the size.'

'Hibernian wolfhound, since you seem be taking such an interest. Her name is Fiedelm, at least I think that's how you pronounce it, and I'm looking after her for a colleague who's currently indisposed. But if you make one quip, just one, about me sleeping with dogs—'

'Desperate times call for desperate measures, Marcus. I'm not one to judge.' She didn't like the way the bloody thing was eyeing her. Not one bit. 'On the other hand, I am sensing an even greater urgency in the matter of our departure, so if you could just grab a tunic and a toga, and perhaps a loin cloth while you're at it—'

'If you're hoping to embarrass me, you're in for a, let's just say, big disappointment.'

'Really? From here, it looks like you prefer the little things in life.'

For a second, she thought the wolfhound was letting out another snarl. Then realized it was Orbilio's deep, patrician laugh. 'In all the time I've known you, Claudia Seferius, I've never taken you for one those bright, young morning people.'

'Would that have anything to do with the fact that I don't like mornings?'

'Or people.' He shot her a sideways glance through the fringe that had flopped over his forehead when he bent down to lace his boots. 'You do know it's not my birthday?'

'I do,' she said. 'But by the time we're through, your career will be so advanced, you'll think it was. With Saturnalia, all rolled into one.'

* * *

Rome wasn't known as the City That Never Sleeps purely on account of the relentless duel between its night-time commercial and day-time industrial activities. Thanks to constant plots to assassinate the Emperor, overthrow the Senate and incite rebellions in the Provinces, it was obliged to keep one eye permanently open. Vigilance was the order of the day.

All the same, nothing in the city ever settled. As Apollo steered his fiery chariot over the rooftops of the Capitoline, the last of the wagons rumbled out through the city gates, their places in the narrow streets instantly filled with porters humping sacks, packs and baskets, schoolboys chanting on their way to lessons, and early bird hucksters setting up their stalls. Already, the braying of donkeys was a distant memory, because now it was the clang of masons' hammers and the cries of water bearers assaulting the eardrums. And let's face it. Although babies never stopped bawling and dogs never stopped yapping, no one seemed to mind now that the air was fragranced with incense from the temples and fresh pies from the vendors, rather than mule shit, sweat and charred torch sticks.

And of course, you can't "just" grab a toga. Never mind the weight, these things are complex, time-consuming garments. Unfortunately, at least for young women being eyeballed by Hibernian demons that came up to their shoulder, no patrician would be seen dead outdoors without one, and, whatever else his faults, Orbilio's blood ran bluer than the Aegean in midsummer. So while he was duly draped and folded, tucked and tweaked, she said, 'Define indisposed.'

Because she'd be, too, if she was forced to look at Fido's beady little yellow eyes day in, day out—

'Fiedelm.'

—tongue hanging out like a limp red flag, and breath that could fell a charging rhino.

'Pretty grim,' he said.

'Fido's breath or its owner's condition?'

'Both.' His mouth turned down. 'The owner's dead. Seizure of the heart, poor fellow, only forty-two. Fiedelm found the body. Sat over it for seven hours, front paws on his chest and wouldn't budge, threatening to savage anyone who came within ten feet.'

'Are you immune to fangs, or did she recognize you?'

It being a colleague's dog.

'You know me. Hide like a crocodile. But in this case, I felt discretion was the better part of valour and decided against putting those long, pointy teeth to the test. Leastways, not on me.' Dogs are dogs, he said, and in the end he lured her away from her master's stiffening body with a lump of greasy bacon. 'A tactic which worked a little too enthusiastically, she's attached herself to me like a limpet, and you know what this means, don't you?'

Claudia felt a sinking in her stomach. 'Oh no.'

'Oh yes.' He was slathering almost as much as the wolfhound. 'Fido's coming with us.'

* * *

Claudia made her third mental note of the morning. That the instant this business with Marcus Cornelius Orbilio was concluded, she was flying straight round to the Temple of Fortune and taking that pendant back. Just so Fortune was clear, it was the lapis lazuli one that slimy linen merchant gave Claudia last week, in the hope of smarming his way into her bed (not to mention her wine business and fortune). Not that it wasn't a beautiful pendant. Indeed, until today Claudia and the goddess had been on pretty good terms—and of all the gods up there on Olympus, this was definitely one Claudia wouldn't want to piss off in a hurry. But if that bitch thought she could set some bloody wolfhound on her, she could kiss goodbye to lapis lazuli, for a start.

* * *

'A bench?'

'My, my, you Security Police are quick on the uptake.'

Marcus stared. 'You woke me at the crack of dawn, dragged me across the seven hills of Rome, then all the way over the Field of Mars to look at a bench?'

'Technically, it could only ever be six hills, since you happen to live on one of them, and it would have been a rather strange and convoluted route to take, don't you think, when we were simply going A to B across the city? Also, we're only halfway along the Field of Mars, in case you'd lost your bearings. But apart from all that, yes. You're absolutely right.'

'A b—'

'Say the word once more and you'll find first hand that it rhymes with wrench, trench and, ultimately, stench.'

He shot her a sideways glance. 'There isn't a grave big enough to hold me.'

'Like Fido's teeth, that might be something else you don't want to put to the test.'

He was, she thought, at his most dangerous when he laughed. As though he was completely ignorant that she was swindling her German, Greek and what were those other ones? oh yes, her Lusitanian customers blind. Or that she was fleecing her suppliers, playing one against the other. And never mind she was committing that most heinous of crimes against the Empire, not paying her taxes. Because don't think I didn't know you, Marcus Cornelius Orbilio. You're stacking up my misdemeanours to throw down, slap, slap, slap, on your superior's desk in a bid to grease your path up the promotional ladder. Make no mistake, she thought. Those dark eyes crinkling at the corners had their sights set firmly on the Senate.

At any cost.

'Tell me, Marcus, what exactly do you see here?'

'Hm.' He walked round it slowly, examining every surface, curve and angle with his eyes and his fingertips. 'I see top quality marble. Parian. The best.'

Flawless, finely grained and so white it was practically translucent, marble from the isle of Paros was almost exclusively reserved for statues.

'I see none of the usual scroll design round the seating. Only perfect, and I do mean perfect, rounded edges. And I see three wide legs to support it, the same Parian marble, with some quite exquisite carvings of lions' heads.' He straightened up. 'Beautiful. In fact, more than that. Exquisite. But no trace of blood, if that's what you're looking for.'

'Me? I'm not looking for anything.' Claudia sat down on the bench, crossed her legs and patted the empty space beside her.

'No, Fiedelm, not you,' he said, pushing the wolfhound aside. For his pains, he was treated to a low, throaty growl, and that's the thing about the Field of Mars. Never a hock of greasy bacon when you need it. 'Ready to tell me what this is all about, Mistress Seferius?'

'What do you see now?'

He shot her a fine-let's-play-games kind of look, but there was no hint of condescension in his voice.

'A nice, green, open space bordering the Tiber, where the military exercise, rain or shine, during the winter months in preparation for battle. And indeed where yours truly used to, not so many years ago.' He paused. 'If I was an owl, I'd swivel my head 180° and tell you all about the oil and wheat and elephants being discharged over at the wharves—'

'Elephants. What a relief, I thought that was Fido.'

'—but since I gave up night flying, my line of vision's reduced to bridges, roads, a couple of theatres. Not forgetting the race tracks frequented by certain young widows sitting not a million miles from me, who make a habit of engaging in illegal gambling activities.'

'I've stopped all that.'

'Of course you have, and I'm sure the only time you attend is when the October Horse is sacrificed. But to continue. If I squint, I can make out one corner of the charming colonnade the Emperor erected in honour of his sister, the odd temple or two, as well as the baths built by the late, great Agrippa. And—' he leaned back '—craning my neck even further, I spy with my little eye four small boys playing soldiers putting up their tents, plus two herons in the boggy grass down by the river.' He straightened up, clasped his hands together and cracked his knuckles. 'More importantly, though, I see your point.'

Benches, for the most part, are the seating of the poor, and usually made of wood. Which is not to say better quality benches can't be found littering the likes of bath houses and the vestibules of temples, and senators and judges also sit on them. With thickly padded cushions, naturally. Equally, it's rare to walk round a rich man's garden without tripping over the wretched things. But—

'Benches of this quality and workmanship are not generally strewn around public places,' Marcus continued. 'Or by people lacking money and influence. This fine specimen has been put here by a rich man for a reason, and you suspect that reason is to watch someone, or something. But more likely someone...'

'But more likely someone,' Claudia repeated quietly. 'Now let me tell you a story.'

* * *

Two weeks earlier, she'd been taking a tour round her peristyle in the hope that the gentle splashing of the fountains combined with the scent of early honeysuckle would somehow inspire a solution to her problem. Because sharp as she was, even Claudia could not attend a banquet thrown by a senator (whose wealth made Midas appear a pauper in comparison, and who—with the right persuasion—might sign up for vast lakes of her exquisite Etruscan wine), while at the same time attend another banquet on the opposite end of the city, thrown by another senator. In his case, wealth was immaterial, though funnily enough, he just happened—with the right persuasion—to be in a position to make at least one of her illegal activities vanish from the record books.

Indeed, so engrossed was she, weighing lucrative orders against slates being wiped clean, that she almost missed the sounds of sobbing in the laurels. At first, she'd taken it to be another case of one of the slaves getting between Drusilla, her blue-eyed, cross-eyed, dark Egyptian cat, and Drusilla's latest garnish for her supper, be it a mouse, a vole, a moth or—if times were hard—a caterpillar. Those claws had exceptionally possessive qualities. On the other hand, there's a vast difference between tears of poor-little-me, tears of pain, and the wracking sound made by someone who's cried so long and so hard, there are no tears left to flow.

'Dear Diana, girl, what's wrong?'

This wasn't one of the slaves Claudia knew personally, the ones who set her hair, fetched her breakfast, polished her jewellery. But she was familiar enough with that mop of bright red hair and upturned nose to know the girl's name was Lydia, she was sixteen years old, an ace with the heather broom, and had been part of her late husband's household before Claudia appeared on the horizon.

'My sister,' she wailed. 'My sister, my sister, my sister…'

Poor kid was so engulfed by grief, her eyes could barely focus. Certainly way beyond the point where she'd question why the Mistress should be kneeling on the ground in front of her, squashing chives and thyme and swathes of blue campanula, and muddying her linen robe as though it was an everyday occurrence. Which meant it took a bit of coaxing—Lydia being virtually incoherent in her distress—but the gist of it was, her younger sister, Alys, had gone missing and, after nearly a week without putting in an appearance, had officially been branded a runaway and put on the slave catchers' list.

'I thought you didn't hold with bounty hunters?' Orbilio said.

'I don't. But Alys, who is only fourteen I might add, isn't one of mine.'

'Ah.'

Ah, indeed. For though the expansion of the Empire holds great appeal for its citizens, those annexed by its endless march don't necessarily hold the same opinion. Rome wasn't entirely autocratic. *Work with us*, they said, *we'll bring you trade, prosperity, roads, protection. You will cease to have enemies that harm you, we will fight your wars for you, and you can keep your gods, your pantaloons, your barbarian tattoos. All we ask in return is your loyalty, observance of our laws – oh, and ten percent of everything that you earn. Which will still leave you with more than you have now.*

Nine times out of ten, the carrot trumped the stick, but there's always one, isn't there? Always one who thinks they can beat the odds. Either out of arrogance. Or because they'd underestimated who (or rather what) they were dealing with. Or they were ill-advised. Or pig-headed. Or, and these were the worst kind, principled.

They, though, weren't the ones who suffered. That fell to the good folk who'd put their trust in their leader. The ones whose crops were destroyed, whose homes were burned, and whose livestock were slaughtered. The poor sods who were tortured if they put up the slightest resistance, their families cut down like wheat at the end of the summer. And when the carnage was over—the message clear to any other tribal leader tempted to follow suit—the raggle-taggle band of farmers and blacksmiths, bakers and bee-keepers that remained would be rounded up and marched to Rome in chains, along with their families, to be enslaved for the rest of their lives. All too often split up on the auction block, on the grounds that division might breed hatred…but it damn well wouldn't breed rebellion.

Of course, their names weren't Lydia or Alys, either, though they'd probably long since forgotten what those names used to be. Once the prisoners of war reached Rome, the little one was despatched with an aunt to a magistrate's house. Lydia being deemed old enough, at the ripe old age of eight, to go it alone, which is when she entered the Seferius household. And where Fortune shone at least a faint beam of light. The houses were only four streets apart.

When our aunt died, almost four years ago, Alys and me became inseparable. Lydia blew her little snub nose on the cloth Claudia gave her, never suspecting it had been torn from the hem of the mistress's gown. *When possible, we'd time our errands so we could meet up. Spent all our free time together, we did. Told each other everything. Which is how I know she never ran off.* Eyes swollen with horror, desperation and fear turned on Claudia. Hands clamped round her wrist. *Alys had nowhere to go.*

'So.' Claudia swallowed. 'I made a tour of the scum who style themselves slave catchers—'

'Bet you went straight to the baths after,' Orbilio said.

'Scrubbed my skin raw and still felt unclean.' She twisted round on the bench to look at him. 'But you know the worst part about this sorry tale? They have six girls around the same age on their lists. Runaways with no reason to run, and those are just slaves. Who knows how many bookbinders, stonemasons, coinsmiths and clerks have daughters who never came home!'

'Hopefully none,' Marcus said. 'My guess is he's targeting slave girls, because no one gives a shit when they go missing. At least, no one who's going to kick up a stink. But I tell you, this bench bothers me.' His arm swept the vista of theatres, boy-soldiers, riverbank and roads. 'The positioning of it makes no sense. For one thing, it's virtually impossible to snatch young women off the Field of Mars in broad daylight. For another how could he possibly know they weren't freeborn?' Most slaves bought their own clothes out of their stipend. 'And last but not least, how many girls are ever on their own here?'

Plenty enough among the entourage accompanying the moneyed classes on their way to the baths, from the baths, taking in the sights, the air, on their way to friends, relatives, even the docks. None running errands or messages, though. That was strictly a job for the boys.

'Lydia asked around, and it seems the magistrate's wife dropped her arm band in the mêlée—'

'Mêlée?'

'This happened during the Megalesian Games.'

Seven glorious days of processions, races and theatrical performances, and while most of the action took place in and around the Circus Maximus, the festivities attracted thousands of visitors into the city.

'The point being that somewhere along the line, the magistrate's wife and her arm band parted company. She despatched Alys to run back and retrieve it, and when the girl didn't return, she simply concluded that the value of a gold snake was too tempting to pass up, that Alys stole the piece and skipped town.'

Orbilio leaned his elbows on his knees and supported his chin with his hands. For several minutes he said nothing. Just let his eyes rove over the wide open space, picturing, perhaps (as Claudia had done), the crush of fishmongers and dentists, sack-makers and tutors entranced by the spectacle of fire-eaters, rope dancers, poets and magicians going through their paces on that cold, crisp, sunny morning…

'Beggars,' he said at last. 'They're all over this Field, whining and keening and calling for alms. They can't all be blind, and you'd be surprised how sharp their memory becomes, not to mention their eyesight, when it comes to a hot quail pie or a bright, shiny coin.'

'Ahead of you on that one.' Her mouth pinched into a narrow white line. 'I've plied them with everything from sausages to wine, honey cakes to pheasant, even scallops right the way from Chios. Hot pies or cold, coins shiny or dull, no one remembers Alys.'

He stroked the dog's muzzle. Ruffled her ears. 'I daresay if she'd screamed, yelled, put up a fight, things might have been different. But a month is a long time to recall nothing out of the ordinary on one of the busiest days of the month.'

Claudia stood up. 'I do hope you're wearing comfortable boots, Marcus. Our walk has only just started.'

* * *

By the end of the day, she'd shown him three more dotted round the Field of Mars, one beside the Temple of Minerva on the Capitol, and another close to the Lupercal, the cave at the foot of the Palatine, where Romulus and Remus were supposedly suckled by the she-wolf. All six benches were the same pure, white, glistening marble, exquisite in the simplicity of their design. All had cost a fortune. And all were close to where the slave girls allegedly ran off.

* * *

His first thought.

Graves.

Dig a ditch, toss a body in, stick a pretty seat on top to draw away attention, the quickness of the hand deceives the eye. But the benches were clean, and relatively new. Any disturbance round the base would show up clearly.

Especially after two weeks of rain.

* * *

Her first thought.

Parallels.

When her father marched off to war and never came home, Claudia was the same age Alys was, when the poor kid's aunt died of fever. The same age Alys was now, when she found her drunk of a mother lying in a pool of congealed blood, from where she'd slashed her own wrists without leaving a note. What Claudia remembered most from that day was the flies. The flies and the terrible, terrible stench. And that is not the last memory of a loved one *any* child should have to carry.

Especially after eight years of pain.

* * *

'One possibility,' Marcus said.

A week had passed, and they were sitting in Claudia's garden, where pinks, honeysuckle and night-scented stocks saturated the warm spring air, bats flitted in and out of the pillars round the peristyle, and stars twinkled like Nubian crystals in the sky.

'That the motive behind the benches was nothing more sinister than the generosity of a wealthy benefactor, offering relief for tired feet on their way in and out of the city.'

'Oh, for heaven's sake.' Having dismissed the slaves an hour earlier, Claudia topped up their wine cups herself. The wine was oaky and dark, full-bodied and rich, reminiscent of the patrician bloodhound beside her. 'I may have my faults, Orbilio, but being wrong isn't one of them.'

'That's what worried me.'

'The fact that I'm right?'

'The fact that I'd be the one to break the news you weren't, and even Fiedelm isn't brave enough for that.'

Light from the sconces reflected gold in the ripples of the pool. The same colour as the beady eyes watching Claudia through a fringe of coarse grey fur. She was pretty sure the message in them was *try me.*

'Which is why,' he was saying, 'I authorized round the clock surveillance on every seat.'

He saw no reason to point out that the role of the Security Police was purely that—to ensure the security of Rome and its Empire—forcing him to fabricate a plot in which conspirators were using Parian marble benches as their meeting point to pass on information. But the fiction was plausible enough to secure him the manpower he needed, and while his boss would have his balls for abuse of position and resources if he found out, his boss wouldn't be kept awake at night by the disappearance of a handful of slaves. *What's the problem? Go out, buy some more, meanwhile hire slave-catchers to bring the runaways home, then punish them in ways that will deter anyone else from even thinking of trying.* The odd thing was, he genuinely believed it was because Orbilio was a snob, that he didn't invite his non-patrician boss round for dinner.

'Now here we are, a week on,' he said, 'and the only thing to show for my troubles is a stream of reports informing me that none of the weary travellers taking advantage of their comfort has shown any abnormal interest in their surroundings.'

'While the sand in the timer's running out, and if we don't find this bastard soon, Marcus, another young girl is going to be written off as a runaway with a bounty on her head.'

He watched the fire in her eyes, which had nothing to do with anger. Anything but. Inhaled her spicy Judean perfume. Wondered why she only let him set foot inside her world when a crime had taken place, when she could trade her help against her illegal activities. As if that mattered a damn. He spiked his hands through his hair. Why couldn't she trust him? After all this time, after everything they'd been through, after he'd proved himself time and again—*why couldn't she bloody trust him?* He let his breath out slowly. What happened to you, Claudia, that the only thing you let close is that banshee of a cat...?

On cue, the banshee dropped down from the balcony on silent paws. Blue eyes met yellow. Both animals tensed. There was a growl, deep and low in the throat. Which didn't come from the wolfhound. Fiedelm, rather wisely in Orbilio's opinion, retreated behind a rosemary bush. Part of him wished that he could join her.

He stared into his wine cup. Watched the light from the sconces bounce off the silver, making the engraved figures round the bowl dance.

'Funny how we all make assumptions,' he said slowly. 'For instance, we assume that when a cat meets a wolfhound standing a yard high at the shoulder, the cat is going to run.'

'Drusilla never backs away from a—mother of Jupiter, you're right! We've been looking at the whole thing the wrong way round.'

The benches hadn't been put in place to watch.

They were put there to remember.

* * *

Question: Assuming their theory was correct and the seats had been set aside for a pervert to wallow in his happy memories, how on earth were they going to identify one man in a city of two million before he struck again?

Answer: Figure out when the next attack would come.

Question: Different locations, different dates, but since such endeavours required meticulous thought and planning, was there a pattern to the abductions?

Answer: Damn right there was. After wading through scroll upon scroll of papyrus, they were able to establish that all six went missing during various festivities. Alys vanished on day five of the Megalesian Games, the others during the Holiday of Mars, the Lupercalia, Saturnalia, the Plebeian Games and the October Horse. Times when everyone from citizens to slaves was happy, relaxed, barely on their guard. And everywhere was thronging. Suggesting the next major festival was the date of his next strike.

Question: How did he know the girls were slaves? They didn't dress differently from, say, a boat-builder or a tavern-keeper's daughter. How could he know the alarm wouldn't be raised when they didn't come home?

Answer: He knew them. This time it was jug upon jug of red wine they waded through before reaching their conclusion, but what other explanation was there? Rich as he was, somehow this man knew the girls, either personally or by sight, which meant he was a regular visitor to their houses. It therefore followed that the girls trusted him enough to go with him. Which meant the bastard stalked them like a lion stalks a zebra. Picking out his target from the herd, before going for the kill—

Question: How in the name of all the gods do you identify such a predator? Rome wasn't exactly short of rich, powerful men making the rounds of banquets, dinners, feasts and festivals at one another's houses. Hell, it didn't even have to be indoors. They mixed and mingled everywhere from the theatre to the Circus, outside temples during ceremonies, at weddings and at funerals, in the Forum, the Basilica, the baths—

'Waste of time, trying to narrow the list of every man who's a regular guest at the magistrate's house,' Marcus said.

Dawn was breaking. Right across the city, cats and clerks would be stretching, chamber pots would be emptied, rumbling bellies would be filled. Here, in Claudia's garden, arrows from Apollo's fiery chariot turned marble statues into gold. Greenfinches trilled out their territories from the tops of the laurels. In the kitchens, bronze pans clanged in almost musical formation, smoke coiled from the boiler room, and, at their feet, Fiedelm snored louder than a herd of fever-ridden hippos.

'I could cross-reference every visitor with men who called at the houses where the other five girls lived, and still have three hundred names to play with.'

It went without saying that his deceitful use of manpower would be withdrawn shortly, too. Sooner or later, his boss would ask for the reports, and with no suspicious activity to show on or around the benches, and not a viable suspect in sight, he would quickly pull surveillance, taking with it Orbilio's last chance of catching a man both he and Claudia were convinced was a cold-blooded killer.

'My men have scoured every inch of this bloody city, questioned every tradesman in the business, every sculptor, every importer of Parian marble, and came up empty-handed every time.'

Which only proved that the benefactor was wealthy enough to bring in private commissions, probably from Greece, and paid handsomely for discretion. No surprises there.

Claudia pinched the bridge of her nose. Yawned the tiredness out of her body. 'Show me those lists again.'

With a hand that felt three times its normal weight, he passed the scrolls across. 'I've been through them a hundred thousand times,' he said. The stubble on his chin was itching like crazy. 'There's nothing there. Not one patrician—not one rich official—not one senator, priest or army general—has so much as rested his arse on those seats for longer than it takes to tie a loose lace on his boot or dig a stone out of his shoe.'

'So what are we missing?' she said.

* * *

Rich or poor, the Ides of May was an important date on everybody's calendar. This was Mercury's birthday, and Mercury was not just the messenger of the gods, he was patron and protector of trade. A cue for thousands of merchants to flood into Rome, all wanting their goods blessed with a quick sprinkle of water from the Winged One's fountain near the Capena Gate to ensure prosperity for the coming year.

In a few weeks, this gate would see wealthy families flocking south through its arches towards the Bay of Naples. Of course, paved roads were originally designed to speed the progress of the military, rather than indolent citizens eager to escape the sticky heat of summer. But all things have consequences, and those paved roads brought commercial expansion on an epic scale. Today, though, its orderly procession of pedestrian traffic had mutated into a seething mass of human ants , each desperate to receive Mercury's blessing. Acolytes could barely keep pace with fumigating the jars with which the water was drawn from the spring, and when the pile of laurel branches to be dipped in the water started dwindling at an alarming speed, it was all the priests could do to keep order.

But when you're trying to isolate one specific grain of sand on the beach, this was an advantage. At least Orbilio could rule out this place as the site of the snatch. Not because the spring was unbelievably public—their predator operated on the principle of "the more blatant the action, the more nobody notices"—but because the crowd was entirely male. Women having their place, all right, just not in business, nudge, nudge, know what I mean? He cast a glance at the exquisitely dressed young woman guarding her wine barrels, who was being constantly jostled to the back of the queue. Claudia Seferius was a thorn in the Guild of Wine Merchants' side, but usually the attacks were furtive and subtle. Today, all bets were off. She was openly talked about, laughed at, scorned and derided. Even humble slave girls would stand out like a sore thumb and be remembered.

* * *

'Mind your backs!'

'I was next.'

'Oi, that was my foot!'

Claudia monitored the clamour beneath a veil pulled low over her eyes. Cheek by jowl in the shade of the adjacent grove of black poplars were her fellow merchants' carts, many perilously top-heavy with merchandise that had either received Mercury's approval or was awaiting it. Hardly the makings for a quick getaway. Especially when the mules would be unhitched until nightfall, when Rome would open its gates once again to wheeled traffic.

Brazen or not, no predator hides its kill in a place where others may find it. Her gaze travelled on.

To the drunk, bumbling around under the trees.

The flute player, hoping to earn a sesterces or two, but losing his rhythm with each bump and push from the crowd.

The rent boy, touting for trade.

All harmless enough, until you remembered that one of Mercury's other jobs was to guide souls down to the Underworld—

'Not this time, pal,' she hissed under her breath.

Not all the merchants brought half their stocks to the spring. Many brought only token samples to be blessed, their litters lined up on the roadside. The drunk blundered over, to the jeer of the bearers, who threw stones at him and mimicked his stumble. At the end of the row, a woman in a pale blue robe was sobbing pitifully into her veil.

'H-have you seen her?' She grabbed the arm of a young girl pushing through with a basket of cold guinea fowl, honey cakes, quail's eggs, warm bread and a chunk of cheese that smelled like it had walked all the way from the Alps. 'Have you seen my daughter?'

'Sorry, ma'am.' The girl shifted her basket to her other arm. 'I haven't seen no one.'

'You must have, oh you must have! She was here. Just a few moments ago. By the gods, I swear I only took my eyes off her for a minute! Will you help me look for my baby girl? Please? She can't be far.'

'Can't, ma'am. Sorry. Only I've got to take this picnic to my mistress, and if I'm late she'll tan my hide—'

'I'm begging you, child, she'll be so scared—I say, don't I know you?' She turned her head towards the only female merchant in the crowd, the object of everyone's attention and derision. 'Isn't that your mistress standing by those barrels? Claudia Seferius?'

The redhead nodded.

'Oh, thank Jupiter! Because I *know* she won't mind if you help me.'

'Well, I—'

'Thank you, child, you are an *angel*. You see, I left my baby girl here, tight beside this litter. I said *don't move*—'

'Funny,' the drunk rumbled in her ear. 'That's exactly what I was going to say.' He combed his hair into place with his free hand. The other was holding a dagger to the woman's throat.

'What do you want? M-money? Jewels? Take them. All of them. This bracelet alone is worth—'

'What I want,' the drunk said, 'is a pure white marble bench.'

'And justice, Marcus,' a voice piped up beside him. The voice was dressed in the kind of clothes a waggoner's, or maybe a fig-seller's, wife might wear. 'Don't forget justice for those six missing slave girls.' Claudia threaded a protective arm round the redhead's shoulders. 'And Lydia, putting herself up as bait.'

'Did I do it right, miss?' Lydia's lip was trembling, her eyes brimming. 'You said move the basket to my other arm when I was approached, no matter who came up—'

'You were perfect,' she assured her. 'Without you, we'd never have caught your sister's abductor.'

'You people are making a big mistake,' the woman warned. 'Just ask that female wine merchant. She'll vouch for me.'

At Claudia's signal, the stand-in turned round.

'You can thank Mercury for that,' she said, tying the woman's hands. 'As if the poor chap hasn't enough on his plate today, he's also god of trickery. But then you know all about that, don't you? Coming in to people's homes—my home—scouting out your victims.'

'If you want to scream, by the way, feel free,' Marcus murmured. 'I'm pretty sure no one in this crowd would notice, another trick you're familiar with, of course. But mainly I'm hoping your struggles will make my dagger slip, because I'd hate to see a sharp point go to waste.'

The tirade of *This is a mistake! An outrage! Don't you know who I am?* cut off in mid-bluster, as she recognized him as the only patrician investigator with the Security Police. 'So help me, I will destroy you, Marcus Cornelius Orbilio. Once the authorities realize who you're dealing with—'

'Authorities?' He frowned. 'I don't remember mentioning the authorities. Claudia, did you hear me mention the authorities?'

'No. Don't think I did.'

'You have an obligation!'

'Indeed I do,' he said.

He didn't mention that it was to the missing girls.

* * *

At that point, particularly when they knew the kidnapper was a woman, hope still pulsed in Claudia's heart. Maybe, just maybe, the girls were alive…? Abducted to order? Perhaps blackmailed into taking them? Even though she was richer than Croesus, it didn't mean she didn't have secrets.

And that's the trouble with hope. It clouds logic. Makes you forget why the bitch spent so much time on the benches. Makes you find excuses for her behaviour, other than sitting there, gloating…

While Orbilio promised amnesty to the litter bearers in return for their co-operation, Claudia prayed with all her heart to Juno, protector of women, that these girls would be found alive, and brought home safe. But her prayers came weeks, in some cases months, too late. The bearers led them to to a warehouse behind a busy wharf. Swore hand on heart they never heard any screams while stationed on guard outside, and, listening to the clatter and the clangs, Marcus well believed them. Their mistress worked on the magician's principle. The more open the action, the less people notice. He insisted on going in alone. When he came out an hour later, ashen-faced and trembling with anger, Lydia dropped to her knees and howled.

'Absolutely no handing this to official channels,' he said thickly.

The State had zero interest in a half a dozen random slave girls, and even if he passed his findings on, the bitch was right. Given that her husband was a senator, a good friend of Augustus, the affair would be hushed up faster than a man could sneeze.

'On the other hand, I'm sure the families of the victims can be persuaded to dispense justice.'

'You can't do that!' The woman's face was white. 'It'll be nothing less than a lynch mob.'

'Only if you're lucky,' Lydia said.

'You won't get away with it. My husband will have people searching for me—'

'Not once he reads your letter,' Claudia said. 'Telling him you're starting a new life with your lover in Carthage.'

Down on the wharf, a tiger snarled in its cage, huge logs of timber were winched through the air, hemp ropes coiled around capstans, sacks of spices were carried down gangplanks and the sun bounced off a tribune's bronze breastplate. Everyone, everywhere, wished Mercury a very happy birthday.

* * *

'If you ever want a job in the Security Police—' Orbilio swirled the wine round in his glass, a lovely piece imported all the way from the Parthian Empire '—feel free to apply any time, Claudia. To say I was impressed with the way you fathomed out the getaway is an understatement.'

Two weeks had trickled by since the Winged Messenger gave his blessing to traders and merchants.

Two weeks since feasting and merrymaking was done in his honour.

Two weeks since he'd guided a killer's cold soul to the Underworld.

'Even more impressed when you pointed out that her litter, permanently at the end of the queue, gave the game away, curtains drawn, bearers still hefting the shafts.'

As opposed to the other crews, lounging against tree trunks, sitting cross-legged on the grass, laughing, drinking, playing dice.

'If she'd chosen the middle, I might never have noticed,' she said. They were in his garden this time. Bigger fountains, taller statues, thicker gilding—that's the aristocracy for you.

'In six lifetimes, I'd never have suspected a woman.' Even when Claudia pinpointed a certain senator's wife spending inordinate amounts of time on the benches, he found it inconceivable that women could be capable of inflicting such cruelty to members of their own sex. Especially ones so pitifully young.

'It's tough being right all the time, Orbilio, but dear me, someone has to do it. Now is it your intendion to let that wine breathe until next summer, or are you going to share it?'

'Your whinge is my command.' He topped up both glasses with a flourish. 'How did you know she'd lure her victims by crying?'

'What stops people in their tracks like nothing on earth? Anguish.' The bitch must have turned it on and off like a spigot.

'Which reminds me,' he said, leaning back and crossing his legs at the ankles. 'You said you discovered Lydia in floods of tears while you were pacing the peristyle, in the hope of figuring out which of two invitations for the same night you should accept. Mind telling me which senator you chose? The one with the contacts, or the one with the money?'

'Oh dear, Marcus, you never change.' She watched moths dance round the flames of the sconces. Listened to the strum of the lyre player tactfully out of sight. 'Always set such horribly low standards, and always fail to meet them.'

As the senator's wife proved on six occasions, curtains on a litter aren't just to keep the sun out, or the rain. They're for privacy.

'My gown was quite the talk of Senator Moneybags' banquet,' she said. 'Such an unusual shade of red, it became something of a competition to put a name to the colour, though you'd be surprised how quickly it blended into a crowd.'

Wine spurted out his nose. 'Would that be because it had already blended out the back door?'

'Admittedly, it became a *little* tedious, changing from red to yellow seven or eight times during the course of the evening, and I refuse to discuss the repercussions of eating two dinners. But on the whole—'

'Being in two places at once brought its rewards?'

'Absolutely.'

If there's one thing Claudia had picked up on her travels, it was that there's no point in having double standards if you don't live up to both. Now then. She smiled prettily. About that smuggling allegation she needed him to make go away…

Beyond the Tree Line

I am not a bad person. I'm not. The general assumption is, if you kill someone, you must be. If the victim's your sister, you're a monster. And if the weapon is poison, then you're evil to the core.

I am none of those things, but I will not lie. The relief after weeks of keeping suspicion at bay—from our parents, her fiancé, the doctor, not to mention Sophie herself—left me wound up tighter than a clock. I needed an outlet, and I needed it badly, but her funeral was hardly the appropriate time. Thus, I trailed my black bombazine with due solemnity along the herb-lined path from St. Osmond's, and if anyone noticed my smile (unlikely, since I'd ordered the thickest, heaviest lace for my veil) well, that was easily justified.

'This scent,' I would sigh. 'Dearest Sophie, speaking to us from Heaven. How she loved pottering with her rosemarys, lavenders and thymes!'

Never mind I'd brushed my crinoline over the plants. People hear what they want to hear, see what they want to see. Precisely how I got away with her murder.

Like a line of black ants, the mourners wound their way inside the Rectory, a crumbling brick monstrosity with wonky thatch, bulging walls and draughty sash windows. I swear the only thing holding it together was the ivy on the walls, a magnet for spiders and flies, and a veritable city for birds, their incessant chirrupping enough to drive a Mormon to drink. But with the curtains drawn, the pendulum out from the clock and every mirror covered, my absence was unlikely to be noticed, and even if it was—

'Poor girl,' they'd say, helping themselves to sandwiches, sherry and scones. 'I'm not surprised she couldn't face the wake. So close, those two. You only have to look at the way Emily nursed her.'

'Heartbreaking.'

'Tragic.'

'Worse for the Reverend and his wife.'

'As if losing their boy in the Crimea wasn't enough, now their beloved daughter, barely eighteen months after.'

Then talk would turn, as it always does, to war, to sacrifice and hardship, heroism and loss, before moving on to politics, and fancy the Queen appointing her prime minister Knight of the Garter when she can't stand the fellow, and for goodness sake, how many times must that scoundrel block the rights of working men to vote, it's a disgrace.

Screened by indignation and shadow, I made my escape, lifted my face to the sun, and breathed in the first day of the rest of my life.

I tell you, freedom smelled good.

In another carefully choreographed move, I slipped into the potting shed, because this is where Sophie spent so much of her time. If anyone saw me, it was only natural I would want to reconnect with her spirit. Sloughing the heavy mourning suit, I set my reticule on top of the crinoline cage and, thanks to Grandmama's trunk in the attic, full of her neatly pressed Regency frocks, the butterfly emerged from its chrysalis.

Hideously old-fashioned with its high bust and puff sleeves, I looked like a milk-maid, but oh my, that muslin was lighter than air. If you can imagine skipping on clouds, that was me.

All the while, the church bell continued to toll.

Half of Melcombe had turned out to pay their respects—whoever imagined my sister was so popular?—another stroke of luck that worked in my favour. There was no one to see me run through the fields, the wind of rebellion strong in my face. One of these days, I will tot up the items on the "not allowed" list. It must surely run into hundreds.

'*…elbows off the table…*'

'*…will you please stop trailing muddy footprints through the house…*'

'*…books live in the book case, Emily, not on the floor…*'

'*…is it too much of an effort to close the piano lid when you've finished…*'

Nag, nag, nag, it's all I ever heard. Not Sophie, you notice. Not Edmond. All the nagging was directed at me. That's because my siblings never stepped out of line, neither would say boo to a goose. But then they weren't free spirits like me, suffocated by rigid rules—and I tell you, I was sick of those rules. Sick, sick, sick of being told not to speak with my mouth full, don't pull the cat's tail, how setting a bag of flour over the door when the Bishop called round wasn't funny. For a man who preached tolerance, Papa didn't practise it much. On and on, on and on with his endless "stop thats", "put it backs" and "how many times must I tell yous?" As I grew older, I'd retaliate by threatening to run off and join the circus, hitch up with a travelling show, or throw in my lot with a band of strolling players, and just in case anyone thought I was bluffing, I'd prop the latest playbill on my dressing table. Take the bones out of that.

Don't go beyond the tree line was well up the list. He insisted it's because there's an old quarry in the woods, overgrown and therefore dangerous, but—

'I've never heard any mention of quarries,' I said to Mama.

'Whether there is or there isn't,' she said, 'you stay clear. Men camp out there. It's not safe.'

'What sort of men?' I asked Edmond.

'Tinkers. Tramps. Prisoners on the run. How would I know?'

Prisoners on the run indeed. The nearest jail was fifty miles away, why would our woods be a magnet for escaped convicts? But this was shortly after he'd got his commission to serve as a captain in the British Army Chaplains' Department, when I suppose it was battle lines that concerned him, rather than tree lines.

My personal theory was gypsies. Brightly clad, fiddle-playing mavericks, their camp full of smouldering beauties in flounced skirts dancing round the fire, while men with gold bands in their their ears sang and clapped. This—THIS—I needed to see, for life was for living, and the only thing I'd known was how to be stifled. I needed to smell stolen meat sizzling on a spit. To be close enough to touch their ornately carved, painted vardos. Peer inside, maybe. I wanted to watch bare-chested men fight for a roaring crowd, blood spurting with every crunching punch. I wanted to be mesmerized by exotic languages and haunting musical instruments. In short, I wanted excitement. Danger. All the experiences that had passed me by—

At the tree line, this glamorous, seductive, perilous tree line, I glanced backwards. The ugly, square church tower in the distance represented my life. Solid, predictable, unchanging, and utterly without character.

Not for much longer, though.

Not for much longer!

This morning's jaunt was a short, but well-deserved treat after the strain of living on tenterhooks. A scouting expedition, if you like, because once I'd established the site of the camp and marked the trail, that I might find it in the dark, I would re-join the mourners and make a special point of comforting Sophie's fiancé. After all, Thomas—Mr. Riddick—was the reason I fed my sister the arsenic, and that, I should stress, was Papa's fault. At least in part. How could he live with himself, instigating her marriage to a handsome stockbroker, at the very time he was palming me off on some sweaty, bald curate? For a man of God, he has a nasty, mean streak, and though she'd always been his favourite, despite my being the youngest, the humiliation was the last straw.

I tied a strip of muslin to the low branch of a tree, which I think might have been ash. I'm not very knowledgeable on these things.

Unlike Sophie, who knew everything about everything.

'The Ancient Greeks used to fashion arrows from ash,' she once told me.

She could only have been nine, and me seven, but I remember it vividly. I'd gone into the kitchen to sneak currants from the jar. Sophie was perched on a stool, sketching Mrs. Shoebridge, the cook, rolling out pastry.

'It's because the wood's flexible and light,' Little Miss Know-All added pompously. 'It doesn't split easily, either.'

'An arrow from the ash will always find its target,' Mrs. Shoebridge said.

Silly woman. You could drown in all her pinch-of-salt-over-the-shoulder, no-opening-umbrellas-indoors, don't-walk-under-ladder nonsense.

'See, when God made the first ash tree, it reached up to Heaven to say thank you, and its boughs spread all over the earth and its roots reached down to the Underworld, which means it can go anywhere it wants now, and that's why an ash arrow is deadly.'

'That doesn't make sense.' I slipped another handful of currants into my pinafore. 'Either there's God and Heaven, which means Hell. Or there are spooky weird spirits—' I waggled my fingers '—ghoulies, ghosties, demons and witches, with secret passageways to Hades.'

'Don't you go mocking what you don't understand, Miss Emily. Ain't no reason there can't be both.' She wagged a flour-covered finger. 'Elm trees is God's markers to the dark world, I know that for a fact, just as the reason holly leaves is prickly is to stop witches running along the tops of the hedgerows.'

The woman was barking mad, of course, but for all that, she made exceptional madeira cakes, delicious crumpets, and her venison pies would make a statue's mouth water.

'On the subject of trees, oak is the one that attracts lightning the most,' Sophie announced, without looking up from her sketch pad. 'So any time you're out in a thunderstorm, Emily, don't stand under an oak.'

Pompous little prig. How she snared Mr. Riddick was beyond me. She was flat-chested for one thing, thin as a rake, her hair was mousy, not fair with ringlets, like mine, and she lacked the comely dimples that pit my cheeks when I smile. More than that, though, she grew from a dull child into a dull adult. If she wasn't pottering in the flower beds, she was raising funds for the poor or doing Good Deeds in the parish, though again, why she felt folk on their deathbeds would welcome visits from her was a mystery.

Don't get me wrong. I'm not unsympathetic. The suffering those poor people go through is horrible, I wish them nothing but peace, and with all my heart I believe they're entitled to every ounce of medical care available to them. I just don't see the point in reading them books, when they won't live to hear the end of the story. And if they were so close to their Maker that they could barely breathe, why spend hours at their bedside, when she could just as easily work on that stupid tapestry in the vicarage, where at least she wouldn't get drenched to the skin on the half-mile walk home.

Equally, I couldn't fathom what Mr. Riddick saw in her. Over time, he'd have come to his senses and realised that piety is just another word for boring, but by then, it would be too late, he'd be married. Thankfully, dear Thomas will never know what a narrow escape he had, or learned the hard way how totally unsuited they were, and right now he was upset, that was natural. Over the course of the next few weeks he'd no doubt visit her grave, bite his lip, lay roses and mutter a prayer. But sustained by my wit, beauty and (dare I say) kisses, he would ride out adversity. What a handsome couple we'd make!

Behind me, the May sun warmed the fields of wheat and barley and put a spring in the step of soft, woolly lambs. Here in the woods, these deliciously dangerous forbidden woods, it dappled the springy ground with dancing, changing patterns, and turned the carpet of bluebells into an ocean. I'd expected silence. Instead, mice, beetles and a thousand other small creatures rustled around in the leaf litter. Squirrels tutted, magpies chattered, pheasants clacked and a woodpecker drummed. What I didn't hear were voices.

Marking the trail with more of Grandmama's muslin, I ventured deeper into forbidden territory, rehearsing the stories I would tell Papa about my nocturnal adventures.

'I thought I heard Sophie singing. I followed the voice…'

'I couldn't believe they welcomed me into their camp…'

'One told my fortune. She said I would marry a wealthy young man, whose heart has been broken…'

Funnily enough, I did have my fortune told by a Romany once. Well, almost! Last summer that was, when a troupe rolled into town with their burton wagons and piebald cobs, a daredevil act with jugglers performing on tight ropes. Ten times more exciting than that Shakespearean company the week before, with their deadly dull *Richard II*, the Romanies brought a fire eater, a sword swallower and a snake charmer in a bright orange turban. Most exotic of all, though, was the tent where Madame Zsa Zsa told fortunes.

'*Kek*,' she snapped, before I even sat down. 'No. I not take black money. You go. *Sherp*.'

'Certainly not, I've been queueing for twenty minutes,' I replied, politely pointing out that my money was anything but dirty. 'I'm the rector's daughter, I'll have you know.'

'Your heart, it is black. I no touch your money. Go, please.'

Obviously this was part of the theatre—like the jangling silver discs round her headscarf, the thick heavy bangles, the crystal ball on the table, the incense—because as I turned, she said, 'Wait.'

I was wrong.

'You.' That was when I saw the fire in her eyes. 'I give you this warning without asking payment, but you.' When she leaned forward, I shivered. 'Be careful.'

Outside, little Miss Gant from the greengrocer's rushed up and grabbed my arm. 'What's she like, this Madame Zsa Zsa? What did she say?'

'The usual.' I laughed it off. 'That I would marry a man in uniform, have six children, and live to a ripe old age. The woman's a fraud.'

Which she was. She probably expected me to go back to my friends, huddling eagerly outside, and relate in goggle-eyed horror the infamous "gypsy's curse"—which naturally would have the opposite effect of putting them off. They would flock in droves to cross her greedy palm with silver. So much for psychic powers, eh? Because unlike Sophie and Edmond, I don't have friends, and not just because no one's ever asked me to join in their various outings and activities, I simply don't need other people. And as for that silly "black heart" nonsense, that's exactly what it was. Tosh. At that point, the thought of killing my sister hadn't entered my head, although I have to say, I was less than pleased when Sophie went running to our parents, telling them how I was glad Edmond wasn't coming home.

That wasn't the first time Mama slapped me, but I tell you now, it was the hardest.

'I didn't say I was glad he *died*,' I wailed, and by heaven, I'd pinch that little tittle-tattle so hard the bruises would still be there at Christmas.

What I'd told her (in confidence!) was that my brother was such a sanctimonious little prude, I was delighted he'd joined up and was out of my hair.

'I *said* it's a relief not to have to listen to his endless progress reports on Mrs. So-and-So's new baby, Mr. Wilkins' gout, whose cat had kittens yesterday, whose horse threw a shoe.'

Right from a young boy, you'd see him scurrying round the Parish at the weekends, after school or in the holidays, delivering messages, carrying shopping, helping out with odd jobs, then relaying every task in vigorous detail over dinner.

'I can't believe he lost his life in the Crimea,' I said, rubbing my cheek. Mama had quite a clout on the quiet. 'From disease, of all things.'

We'd never know which, given that seventeen thousand British troops succumbed to typhus, dysentery or cholera out there, five times the number killed in action, what a desperate waste of life. Hand on heart, the last thing I wanted was for Edmond to die, much less alone and a long way from home, and while I was annoyed with Sophie for both distorting and betraying my confidence, telling tales isn't motive for murder. Also, back then Mr. Riddick was simply the son of Papa's old school chum who came to visit, along with his father. That he and my sister rubbed along was pleasing in the extreme, and by the time they announced their engagement, I was very much looking forward to meeting the young gentleman Papa had lined up for me. My father might be strict, but clearly he had good taste in beaus!

Watching the trail of ribbons dance in the breeze, I inhaled lungfuls of earthy, damp air, while birds sang and butterflies flittered. I'd been gone less than half an hour, yet already the Rectory was a lifetime away. A little further, I decided. Rebellion was too exhilarating an experience to cut short—and as for quarries, tramps and convicts, I could see this was another invention designed to chain my free spirit.

Sorry to disappoint you, Papa.

This spirit cannot be chained.

Certainly not to a balding curate two inches shorter than me, no matter how attentive and sweet. He'd walked beside me as we followed the hearse that carried Sophie on her final journey round the town. Put his little clammy hand on my shoulder as they lifted her coffin and carried it into the church.

'You're very brave,' he whispered.

Poor curate misunderstood my stillness. What he believed was me staring down my grief was in fact me staring at the horses in the harness. Perfectly trained. Not a twitch. Not a snicker. My sister (and there is irony here) would have patted their noses, stroked their shiny black manes, ruffled the feathered plumes on their heads, all the while informing me that while the average age of a horse was twenty, many lived to twice that, and did I know that behind those blinkers were the biggest eyes of any land mammal, with virtually 365° vision?

Like I said, Sophie knew everything.

She knew that Lady Jane Grey, Tudor queen for nine days, used to read Plato. She knew why the sands of the Sahara sing—something to do with vacuums between the moving sands on top and the stable sand below, if I recall. She knew the tongue of a giraffe is more than eighteen inches long. She knew quaking bogs were formed from sphagnum moss. She knew she'd contracted cholera, because even though the worst of the nationwide epidemic had passed, outbreaks were still common, and it spread round Melcombe's poor like wildfire.

She knew everything, did my sister. Everything except how I slipped arsenic into her food, then spoon fed her to make certain, and in a way, it's a shame I couldn't have consulted her on the subject. Would have saved the poor thing a great deal of suffering, as I experimented with crushed cherry pips and greengage stones with unpleasant but far from fatal effect.

Then William Palmer became headline news. Nicknamed the Prince of Poisoners by the press on account of ten suspected murders, he was prosecuted for only one, found guilty, and was hanged. Antimony, strychnine, ammonia—he may have been a thief, a gambler and a mediocre doctor, but you couldn't fault the skills he'd picked up as a chemist's apprentice. Greed was his downfall. He killed his mother-in-law for the inheritance. His wife for the life insurance. His five children for the financial burden they incurred. It was only when he killed his best friend for his winnings that the police cottoned on. Goodbye, William Palmer.

I am not greedy.

Sophie was already dying from the same cholera pandemic that had claimed twenty-three thousand souls across Britain. You could see it in her sunken eyes, wrinkled skin and watery evacuations.

I did not set out to kill her.

I merely wished to ease her path, and if that happened to open a door to a life of satins and soirées with a handsome stockbroker, who wouldn't take advantage?

You might argue that arsenic is no way to ease that journey. I disagree. Mr. Palmer's mole-like eyes staring out of *The Melcombe Tribune* reminded me how there were kinder alternatives to hastening death than ground up cherry stones, and arsenic was one. How simple to sneak rat poison from the stables when the groom went for lunch.

Oh dear, these woods. Crows, cuckoos, chiffchaffs and jays, weasels, wood mice and stoats. No gypsy fiddles, though. No whinnying cobs. No barking of dogs. Not even—despite my disappointment, I smiled— the rattle of an escaped convict's chain! Time to turn back, because while the Romany daredevils didn't return, the strolling players were performing in *Midsummer Night's Dream* tomorrow. It might be presumptuous, but I'd slipped the playbill in my reticule before we left for the funeral. Mr. Riddick would need a diversion to take him out of himself, and a light play struck me as just the ticket. In fact, the sooner he came to rely on me for comfort and support in his hour of grief, the better. Then one thing would lead to another, so no. Not presumptuous. Merely sound planning.

Gosh! Trailing the hearse around Melcombe, then the funeral, followed by this little adventure had quite taken it out of me. I leaned against the trunk of a tree to catch my breath, and this one I knew. Everyone did. Yew trees were dotted all round St. Oswald's churchyard.

Don't touch the berries, they're poison, Papa said.

Honestly, who'd want to?

'Guardian of the Underworld, the death tree's immortal.' Lord alive, when it came to old wives tales, myth and superstition, no one could match Mrs. Shoebridge! 'Older than Christ, some of them yews in the graveyard.'

'This from the woman who thinks birches adopt female form on full moons,' I snorted to Sophie. 'I'll bet she nicked *her* toes a few times on the tops of the holly!'

'You can see where the idea comes from,' Sophie said. 'The branches grow downwards to form new trunks in the earth. These twist together to envelop the old trunk. That rots. More branches grow. I suppose when you look at it that way, the yew really is the closest thing to immortality.'

Immortal? Hardly. Comfortable? Most definitely.

Now, of course, it was Sophie who was immortal. Forever that young woman gazing wistfully out of the silver frame on the mantelpiece, the rose in her hair never wilting. Strange how fate conspires. If she hadn't insisted on visiting the poor, she wouldn't have contracted the cholera, and I wouldn't be planning theatre trips with Mr. Riddick. Perhaps it should have been *All's Well That Ends Well* they were putting on?

Right then! Time to retrace my dangling blue trail to the tree line, but there was the funny thing. When I tried to haul myself off the trunk, I could not. Literally, physically, I could not move. In a cloud of panic, yet at the same time ice cold clarity, I understood the expression "rooted to the spot."

The yew tree—the death tree—had claimed me.

And now it was pulling me in, covering me with its bark. I couldn't scream. Couldn't call. I was frozen in body but not in mind. This was wrong. WRONG. I'm not a bad person. I don't deserve this. I deserve happiness, light, a chance to be free and let my true spirit shine! Those soirées and silks? *They* are my future. Not one in which I'm terrified, powerless, trapped rigid, upright and invisible for ever. The Romany's warning washed over me.

'You,' she said. 'Be careful.'

Only she didn't say that. She said yew.

'Yew. Be careful.'

As my mind fought in the way my body could not, I knew there would be no tidal wave of tears falling from my parents, the way they had for Sophie. My mother would not be on her knees, howling like a wild animal, the way she was for Edmond. Thomas would still think of himself as Mr. Riddick when it came to his fiancée's sister, the cook would still be citing tree lore to anyone who'd listen, and like I said, I don't have friends. Papa would find my mourning clothes alongside the "dressing up" trunk in the potting shed, see the strips of muslin leading nowhere in the woods, and believe his daughter had set up a Midsummer Night's whimsy of her own, before running away with the strolling players as she'd threatened endless times before. The proof was the playbill in her reticule, left on top for everyone to find.

All the same, in a hundred and sixty-five long years, I hoped I'd hear at least one person call my name.

Cover Them with Flowers

Below the majestic peaks of Mount Parnon, Night sloughed off her dark veil and handed the baton of responsibility to her close friend, the Dawn. Daughter of Chaos, mother of Pain, Strife, Death and Deception, Night continued her journey. Gliding on silent, star-studded feet towards her mansion beyond the Ocean that encircled the world. Here she would sleep, until Twilight nudged her awake and her labours would begin all over again.

At the foot of the temple steps, Iliona rinsed her fingers in the lustral basin, carved from the finest Parian marble, and lifted her face to the sun. In the branches of the plane trees, the bronze wind chimes tinkled in the breeze. White doves pecked at the crumbs of caraway bread that was baked daily, especially for them. Whether the seeds were addictive, or the pigeons were simply content with their lot, the High Priestess had no idea. But the doves rarely strayed from the precinct, and it wasn't because their wings had been clipped.

Another few minutes and the first of the workers would start to arrive. Scribes, libation pourers, musicians and heralds. Basket bearers, janitors and the choirs. Every day was the same. They would barely have time to change into their robes before the sacred grounds were swamped with merchants, wanting to know if today was the day they'd grow rich. Wives, desperate to know if last night's efforts had left them with child. The poor, fearful of what lay ahead. Cripples would flock to the shrine, seeking miracles. The sick would come seeking cures. Wisely or not, Iliona had taken it upon herself to interpret their dreams, sometimes the behaviour of birds, even the shapes of the clouds, to give them the peace that they needed.

But for now—for these precious few minutes—that peace was hers, and she basked in its solitude. The soft bleating of goats floated down from the hills. Close at hand came the repetitive call of a hoopoe. Letting the sun warm her face, she breathed in the scent of a thousand wildflowers carried down from the mountains and over the wide, fertile meadows. Narcissus, crown daisies, crocus and muscari… along with, unless she missed her guess, a faint hint of leather and woodsmoke.

'I'm beginning to think the rumours are true,' she said without turning round. 'That the *Krypteia* never sleeps.'

'You should know better than to listen to gossip,' chided the leather and woodsmoke through a mouth full of gravel. 'I sleep.' He paused. 'Upside down in a cave, admittedly. Cocooned in my soft velvet wings.'

The hair at the back of her scalp prickled. If the Chief of Sparta's Secret Police was making jokes, it must be serious.

'What can I do for you, Lysander?'

Had he discovered that she was still aiding deserters? A crime punishable by being blinded by pitch and thrown, bound and gagged, in the Torrent of Torment. Or that she was rescuing deformed babies that were thrown over the cliff…? Slipping food to prisoners in the dungeons…?

'Me? My lady, I wouldn't dare to presume.' His voice was slow and measured, but the teasing note was unconcealed 'Your country, on the other hand would be immensely grateful for your input and wisdom.' He cleared his throat, instantly changing the mood. 'Three women have been found hanged.'

Now she turned.

'*Three?*' But for all the shock, what was uppermost in Iliona's mind was that he looked older than the last time they'd met. The lines round his eyes were as deep as plough furrows, and there were more silver strands framing his temples. On the other hand, his short, warrior kilt showed no weakness of thigh muscle, and his chest still put a strain on the seams of his tunic. 'On the same night?'

'Same night, same house,' he said, explaining how they were three generations of the same family. 'Girl of fourteen, her mother and grandmother. And as much as I would like to dismiss this as some eccentric death pact, or even double murder followed by suicide, there were no stools that could have been kicked away. No chairs, no tables, no blocks of wood. Nothing.'

Small wonder he looked weary. However feared and hated the Secret Police, when it comes to women being strung up like hams, even the toughest among them are affected.

'It's no mean feat to creep into a household, overpower three women and hang them,' she pointed out. There would be servants. Dogs. Any number of obstacles.

'The alarm horn wasn't blown,' he said. 'In fact, there were no signs of a struggle in or outside the house.'

Which might, she mused, be because the killer was cunning enough to cover his tracks. Or maybe obsessively tidy—

Now that acolytes had begun milling round the precinct, lighting the incense in the burners and sweeping the steps with purifying hyssop, Iliona suggested a stroll down to the river. Here, shaded by willows and poplars, they would able to speak without being overheard. Gathering up her white pleated robes, she found a perch on a rock and watched a heron stalk the lush grasses on the far bank for frogs, while moorhens dabbled in and out of the rushes and butterflies fed off the thistles. The river was at its fullest, thanks to the snowmelts, but the Eurotas was one of the few rivers in Greece that didn't dry up in high summer. That's why the river god was so revered by the people, and why so many flocked to his temple.

Why peace was so hard to come by.

'This is a monstrous crime, truly it is. But I don't understand why the *Krypteia* is involved.'

Unless the victim was royalty or a member of the Council, murder was hardly the preserve of the Secret Police. Much less its ruthless commander.

'Two reasons.' Lysander picked up a pebble, dropped to one kilted knee, and skimmed the stone over the water. Flip-flip-flip, eight times it jumped. But then everyone jumped for the *Krypteia.* 'Primarily, this triple murder will send shock waves round Sparta, and I need to neutralize the situation before it undermines morale.'

To remain the strongest land power in Greece, Sparta had turned itself into a nation of warriors, with boys joining the army at the age of seven. In the barracks, they would learn the values of endurance through discipline, hardship, deprivation and pain, pushing their bodies to limits that most men couldn't stand. Not for nothing was the mighty Spartan army feared wherever it went. But with the men away, protecting smaller and weaker city states from being gobbled up by their neighbours, they had every right to expect their womenfolk to be safe. Murder had suddenly become a political issue.

'Also.' Flip-flip-flip, another eight times. 'This was the family of one of my generals.'

'And naturally you owe it to him, to bring the culprit to justice?'

'Not exactly.' His smile was as cold as a prostitute's heart. 'This man is after my job, and I don't intend to give him a reason to get it.'

Iliona watched the swallows dip over the river for flies. Smelled the wild mountain thyme on the breeze. 'What has this to do with me?'

Something twitched in his cheek. 'Who else sees through the eyes of the blind, and hears the voice of the voiceless? You count the grains of sand in the desert, and measure the drops in the ocean.'

She jumped to her feet.

'How dare you mock my work! You know damn well that the poor, the weak, the dispossessed and the lonely come to this temple because they need something to lean on. Well, the support I give them is solid and sound, and it matters this—' she snapped her fingers '—that my oracular powers are fake. I set riddles, Lysander, in order that these people can find the solutions to their problems themselves, and don't get me wrong. These murders are tragic.' Desperately so. 'But since I don't know the women, I have nothing useful to contribute. On this occasion, I am unable to help you.'

Without pausing for breath, she rattled off a long list of tasks that could not be abandoned. Oracles aside, who would preside over the endless rituals and sacrifices? Dispense oaths in the name of the again river god? Log donations and offerings in the various treasuries?

'The altars would not be properly purified, there are mountains of letters to dictate, and let's not forget the accounts that need overseeing, the various marriages and funerals that needed officiating, and not least, the preparations for the forthcoming spring carnival.'

'Hm.'

For a long time he said nothing. Just kept flipping pebbles over the water. She waited. Baiting him might be argued as the height of stupidity, but if he had come to arrest her, he would have done it by now. A girl had her pride, after all! At the same time, High Priestesses aren't exactly naïve. She knew it was only a matter of time before he resorted to blackmailing or bullying her into co-operating, as he had so many times in the past. Even so, she had no intention of making it easy for him, and job security wasn't her problem. In fact, many more deserters would be helped, babies rescued, prisoners comforted, with a new man at the helm of the *Krypteia.* One who did not know her past.

So it came as a surprise when Lysander rose to his feet and said quietly, 'That is your answer?'

She squared her shoulders. Wondered what pitch smelled like, when it was close to the eyes. 'It is.'

'Then I bid you a very good day, Iliona.' He placed his fist on his breast in salute. 'May Zeus bring you all that you wish for.'

A chill ran from her tiara to her white sandalled toes. He was a fighter, a warrior, a leader of men, who used every weapon in the book to win and get what he wanted. The Head of the Secret Police did not back down. He was up to something, the bastard.

'Wait,' she called, but he'd already gone.

Fear crawled in the pit of her stomach.

* * *

Night rose, slinking through the Gate of Dreams, to work again her dark powers over the earth. The days passed, the nail on the wall calendar marking their journey, highlighting those days which were propitious for planting, those which were auspicious for building, as well as those which cursed folk for telling lies. Not once did Iliona stop looking over her shoulder, but, as time passed, she began to relax.

Sacrifices were presided over with ritualist precision, oaths were dispensed in the name of the river god, donations and offerings were logged in the various treasuries. The altars were purified. Properly, of course. Those mountains of letters were duly dictated, the accounts managed with customary efficiency, and, thanks to the High Priestess's efforts, the spring festival went off without a hitch. Even the procession of children, carrying cakes stuck with burning torches, managed to reach the sacred pine tree without anyone tripping up. Usually at least one child would set fire to the carpet of needles, and last year the bee-keeper's daughter exceeded all records, setting the harp player's tunic alight as she stumbled, then singeing his hair when the poor man tried to stamp out the flames.

'You're working too hard,' said the Keeper of the Sacred Flame, one of the few true friends Iliona had.

'It's the season,' she lied. 'Everything comes at once in the spring.'

And to prove it, she went off to burn incense.

'You're not sleeping,' observed the temple physician.

'It's the season,' she shot back. 'The nights are too hot.'

And to prove it, she walked round wafting a fan.

As for the triple murders, the entire State was indeed sickened by the slaughter of three defenceless women. What kind of monster would do this? And yet, thought Iliona, in a country of full-time professional soldiers who virtually lived at the barracks, Spartan women were strong. How was it possible to overpower three at the same time?

As well as horrific, she found the crime deeply unsettling.

Being a second cousin to the king, she had many contacts at the palace and, through them, kept abreast of events. She learned, for instance, that, with typical *Krypteia* thoroughness, Lysander's agents had explored every avenue in their attempt to bring the killer to justice. Could this have been a grudge killing, to punish the husband? Goodness knows, an uncompromising general collects enemies like a small boy collects caterpillars. Except there was nothing in his military history to point to a need for such dire retribution, nor in his personal life. Was the wife having an affair which had soured, inspiring the lover to take revenge? Apparently, running the farm in the general's absence left no time for romance, had the mother-in-law upset someone? Again, this was ruled out— but the daughter? Wasn't she engaged to be married next year? What about the family of the future in-laws? Was there someone who didn't approve of the political union? At the time of the killing, the general was heading an assault in the Thessalian hinterland, making his alibi more solid than iron. Which was not to say he couldn't have paid an assassin to wipe out his womenfolk. But why would he???

Through those same contacts, Iliona read the reports of every interview and interrogation that had been conducted, and monitored the leads on the literally dozens of suspects. Consequently, she grew as frustrated as the investigators, since everyone and yet no one was in the frame for these murders. Was one woman the target, she asked herself? Forcing the killer to silence the others after his crime was discovered? But why hanging? Why in a line…?

Meanwhile, life at the Temple of Eurotas continued on its daily course of setting riddles, interpreting dreams and committing enough treasonable offences to tempt Iliona to blind herself with pitch and save the authorities the trouble. Out across the valley, the buds on the vines uncoiled into leaf. Willows were cut to be woven into baskets, the olive trees were pruned back, oxen were gelded, and thousands of baby birds hatched. But as the spring progressed and the nestlings left home, the killings continued to dance at the back of her mind.

As did the shadow of the *Krypteia.*

⋆ ⋆ ⋆

A month to the day after Lysander's visit, Iliona was at the house of her cousin, Lydia. Now in most city states, the decision to expose weak or deformed babies was the preserve of the father, thus leaving a certain amount of room for manoeuvre. In Sparta, however, where virtually every male citizen was a warrior of one kind or another, this decision was down to the State. And the State liked to decide very early on whether his little limbs looked like they would grow straight enough to grow up and march thousands of miles in full battle dress. Or whether he had a good, loud bawl, indicating that he would eventually be strong enough to throw spears and go hand-to-hand with the enemy. Those who failed the test were taken to the Valley of Rejection up in the mountains and thrown into the abyss.

Little room for manoeuvre in that.

Unless, of course, someone happened to have a fishing net rigged up and ready to catch them. Someone who, when the little mite was hurled into space, was also on hand to heave a blanket-covered stone into the gorge. One that made the right kind of thud when it landed.

The State called it treason. Iliona called it giving childless artisans the family they craved.

Aware that, one of these days, her luck would run out.

But for now, the sun shone on the jagged peaks of Taygetus, still capped in snow, and the Hoeing Song drifted on the breeze from the men working the fields. Lydia's husband, like the rest of the army, was off fighting someone else's battles, an annual exodus which, with spectacular regularity, sparked a glut of babies nine months after their return. Another reason why the fathers did not make that all-important decision. They weren't here.

'Who's a bonny boy, then?'

Iliona cradled the infant in her arms, while Lydia sat in the corner, grey-faced and shaking with fear. Her son was not deformed, but, arriving eighteen days before his due date, he was certainly a weak little baby. Now, five days after the birth and in accordance with the law, the Elders had gathered at the family shrine in the courtyard to pass judgment on the strength of his bawl.

'They're going to take him.' Lydia had no doubts. 'My baby, my only child, and they're going to reject him.' Tears trickled down her face. 'Suppose I'm unable to bear more children? Suppose— '

'Dry your tears,' Iliona said softly. 'I have cast the runes, read the portents and heard the voice of the river god dancing over the pebbles. Eurotas does not lie, Lydia. You will watch your son grow into a man.'

Runes and pebbles be damned. What didn't lie was the phial of willow bark infusion secreted in the folds of her robes.

'Gentlemen.'

Making ritualistic gestures to disguise the bitter liquid that she dripped on his tongue, Iliona handed the baby over for inspection.

'By Hera,' gasped the astonished Elders. 'They will hear this little man in Athens!'

Consequently, the celebrations were especially fierce, with flutes and trumpets, singing and laughter, and wine flowing freer than midwinter rain.

Which made the herald's announcement all the more shocking.

'On the road to Messenia, just beyond the fork,' he said, 'the bodies of three women have been found, hanging from the beams of their farmhouse.'

Daughter, mother, grandmother. Exactly as before.

* * *

Surrounded by olive groves on one side and paddocks on the other, the farm's main output was barley, where field after field of feathered stalks rippled in the warm, sticky breeze. Another week, two at the most, thought Iliona, spurring her stallion up the dusty track, and the crop would be ready for harvesting. Making it all the more poignant that the women would not see it.

Reining her horse as she approached the buildings, she glanced along this green and fertile valley. Enjoying a better climate than most of Greece, and with a constant flow of water, Sparta was not only self-sufficient, but in a position to export large quantities of grain and livestock. Add on a lively trade in iron, porphry, racehorses and timber, and it was easy to see why the State had grown so rich. Of course, like everyone else, land ownership was only available to citizens, just as tax was deemed too degrading for men who put their lives on the line every day. Instead the State taxed the artisans who made their armour and weaponry. And did so without ever seeing the irony of that decision.

'I'm surprised the temple can spare you,' Lysander drawled, coming out of the house to meet her.

Iliona tethered her stallion beside the water trough, shook the red dust off her robes and thought, if he expected her to apologize, he was in for a long wait. 'May I see the murder scene?'

She expected him to make another sarcastic comment, possibly along the lines of surely she, who could see through the eyes of the blind, had seen it in the sacred bowl? Instead, he ushered her past the porter's lodge and through the atrium in silence. Country villas were pretty much the same in design, being built around a central courtyard with a colonnade running round the sides. What differentiated them was the lavishness of the frescoes, the quality of the stone, the lushness of the couches and the richness of the tapestries on the walls. There was little of that here. A hoplite's family, not a lofty general's. A family who were scraping to get by.

'Are you sure you want to go in?' Lysander paused at the entrance to the store room to light an oil lamp. 'We haven't cut them down yet.'

We? As far as Iliona could tell, there was no one else here. In the hush, she could smell vinegar, honey and olive oil, and, when he lifted the lamp to light the way through the archway, she noticed that the air was hazy with flour.

'Yes.' She nodded. 'I'm sure.'

She wasn't. Far from it. But if she'd gone with Lysander one month before, maybe these women would still be alive. Facing them was the least she could do.

'Your frown tells me something strikes you,' he said, setting the lamp on the shelf.

'The distance between them.' It was the first thing she'd noticed.

After the obvious. 'The spacing between each noose is almost identical.'

'Not almost.' He held up both hands so that his thumb-tips met, then splayed his fingers. 'Exactly three spans between each rope, just like last time.'

'You didn't tell me that at the temple.'

'I believe you were busy.'

Chip, chip, chip. He wasn't going to let her forget her refusal to help, and frankly, she didn't blame him. 'Still no witnesses?'

'The farm doesn't employ many labourers, and those they do live in huts in the hills.'

'But three women,' Iliona said. 'I mean, look at them. They're hardly pale, puny creatures.'

The grandmother had arms like a blacksmith's, the mother's legs were like tree trunks, and even the girl, not yet fourteen, was a strapping young thing.

'They wouldn't be mistaken for Athenians, that's for sure.' He almost smiled. 'However, one thing is certain.' The smile hardened into a grimace. 'I won't bore you with detail, but if there's one thing I know, Iliona, it's death. These poor bitches were alive when they were hanged.'

Yet there were no scratched fingers, from where they'd clawed at the rope. No dishevelled clothing. Just dolls hanging, three in a row. All evenly spaced. 'He drugged them,' she said.

'That would be my guess.' Lysander rubbed at his jaw. 'After which he either dragged or carried them here to the store room, but if you look around, the herbs on the floor to deter vermin are intact.'

'More likey they've been brushed back into place.'

The killer was as she'd suspected. Tidy to the point of obsession. Worse, he was cunning, careful and intelligent with it. She cast her eyes over the various sacks and amphorae lined up round the storeroom. That was what Lysander had been doing when she arrived. Untying, unstoppering, sniffing and testing. Hence the fusion of smells in the air. He obviously hadn't found anything pertinent, though. More a question of thoroughness than anything else.

'Aah.' Her mouth pursed in compassion as she picked up a small wooden daisy among the dried stalks of rosemary, tansy and lemon balm beneath the daughter's feet. 'This was probably her lucky charm, which fell out of her clothing when—'

'Let me see that!' Lysander snatched at the lantern for a closer look, and then swore. A short, sharp, vicious expletive.

'What is it?' she asked, because suddenly he was scrabbling around beneath the other two bodies, swearing harder than ever.

'I found a carved rose on the floor of the first house,' he said. 'Right below the mother, but—' More expletives. '—didn't give it a thought.' He held out three carved flowers, one under each of the bodies in the storeroom. A daisy, a rose and a lily. 'How could I have been so stupid?'

His anger pulsed through the windowless room as if it had substance and form.

'How could you have imagined it was anything other than trivial?' she replied. 'I also dismissed it.'

But Iliona was not the *Krypteia*. The *Krypteia* don't make mistakes…

'I need to re-visit the first scene,' he spat.

As it happened, the house had hardly been touched in the month since its occupants were ferried across the Styx to the land of the shades. In no time, he'd recovered three wooden flowers among the strewing herbs on the floor.

A daisy, a rose and a lily.

⁎ ⁎ ⁎

The moon was full, dulling the starlight, as Iliona stood in the clearing in the hills. Twinkling silver far below was the river whose god she served, and whose annual floods brought wealth and plenty. It took an hour to cross the valley by foot, but three days to travel its length on a horse. Through olive groves, barley fields, paddocks and vineyards. A tranquillity that was now broken, thanks to one man. A monster.

In the two weeks since the second murders, the general had been pushing hard for Lysander to step down. His incompetence had led to a reign of terror, he'd stormed to the Council, and Iliona could only imagine the grief and despair that was churning inside him. With his family wiped out, anger was all he had left.

Which was better, though? For the Secret Police to be led by a man whose impulses were driven by blinding emotion? Or an honourable man, who would not baulk at blinding her with pitch before throwing her into the Torrent of Torment? She stared at the rugged tracks criss-crossing this red, stony land like white scars in the moonlight. Smelled the pungent moss under her feet. Listened to a stream frothing its way downhill, over the rocks. With their dark cliffs and secret caverns, these mountains were at once dangerous, beautiful, treacherous and magnetic. No different from Lysander himself.

But how do you define beauty? The scent of dog rose had suddenly become cloying. The sight of daisies made her feel sick.

She listened to the music made by the squeaking of bats and the soft hiss of the wind in the oaks. If only she could unravel the significance of those flowers! Of the spacing between the nooses! Of choosing three women of the same family…

A twig snapped. She looked round. Knew that, if he wanted, he could have crept up and not made a sound. The smell of woodsmoke and leather mingled with the aromas of moss and wild mountain sage, and in the moonlight his eyes were as hard as a wolf's. She wondered how Lysander had found her hiding place. And whether he'd seen the deserter she'd just helped to escape…

'Would you believe my orders—' He leaned his back against a tree trunk and folded his arms over his chest. '—are to identify and protect every household that fits the pattern for the killings.'

An impossible task. Sparta currently had three thousand warriors scattered all over Greece, every last one of them landowners, and given that they were all aged between eighteen and thirty, probably two thirds had widowed mothers and daughters living at home. Their sons, of course, would be in the barracks, while the older men, retired veterans, were either working their own farms or employed in auxiliary military work. Obviously people were keeping an eye on their neighbours, while remaining vigilant themselves. But spring was a busy time on the land. The *helots* who worked it needed close supervision, or they would rise up and rebel, or take off.

'The general hates you,' she said.

'He holds me responsible.'

'Either way, he's engineered it so that you will either fail in your efforts to protect every woman in Sparta, or be forced to disobey orders.'

His lip twisted. 'Providing I can put a stop to this murdering sonofabitch, the Council will forget that I challenged their authority.'

The deserter… Fifteen years old… Was he already lying in a gully with his throat slit?

'The moon,' Iliona said, wondering if Lysander's dagger was still warm from the boy's blood. 'The moon has three phases. Waxing, full and waning.'

'Three women!' He jerked upright. 'Also waxing, full and waning!'

'Exactly. And all killed at the new moon.' Iliona dragged her eyes away from his scabbard. Straightened her shoulders, and swallowed. 'Suggesting the daughters might be the key.'

'To what?'

'I don't know,' she admitted. 'But how in the name of Zeus did he manage to drug them?'

'That second family,' Lysander said slowly. 'He had to have drugged them out in the courtyard, otherwise he would have strung them up from the beams in the kitchen like the first three.'

'You think the killer might have been a guest?'

Whoever he was, he was a coward who craved power. And could only get it when his victims couldn't fight back.

'Our investigations haven't turned up any visitors, and don't forget, the first trio. Not many guests are entertained in the kitchen.' Lysander clucked his tongue. 'Not at the general's level.'

'What about wood carvers?'

'What about them? There are hundreds inside the city alone, and none of them sell flowers like the ones placed under the bodies. As a trade, it fits your theory of precise, intelligent and tidy. Then again, every man and boy who's ever owned a knife — which is everyone — has had a go at carving at some stage.'

Needles and haystacks, needles and haystacks.

Would this monster ever be caught?

* * *

Two weeks later, when the new moon scratched her silver crescent in the sky, Iliona found her answer. In a house deep in the artisan quarter, three more women were found dangling, with the same flowers under their feet. The daisy, the rose and the lily. Now the terror was palpable. These were not exalted citizens. Landowners and farmers. They were tradespeople. The family of a humble harness-maker, who was away in Thrace, supporting the cavalry.

But that wasn't the worst of the matter. Three days before the moon was due to rise, the women brought in supplies and barricaded themselves indoors. No one had been allowed in, they wouldn't even open the shutters, and the alarm was only raised when their neighbour, an Egyptian gem-cutter, could elicit no response. He and the wheelwright broke down the door.

This, obviously, was the work of no human hand.

Sparta had angered the gods.

* * *

'Bullshit.' Lysander paced the flagstones of Iliona's courtyard, spiking his hands through his long warrior hair. 'Complete and utter bollocks.'

While he prowled, Iliona sat on a white marble bench in the shade of a fig tree, surrounded by scrolls of white parchment.

'I agree.'

The gods controlled the weather, the seasons, human fate and emotions. That was why they needed to be propitiated. To ensure fruitfulness, justice, victory and truth, and offset famine, tempest and drought. True, Deception wove her celestial charms while men slept, as did Absent-mindedness, Panic and Pain. But so did the Muses, as well as Peace, Hope and Passion, and the goddesses of beauty, mirth and good cheer.

'All the appropriate sacrifices have been made,' she continued.

To Zeus, a ram purified with oak. To Poseidon, a bull, another to Apollo, honey cakes to Artemis and grain to Demeter. The gods had no reason to argue with Sparta.

'Also, the Olympians might take life, but not in this way,' she added. 'They kill, but they do not leave flowers.'

'If we knew what it meant, this daisy, roses and lily business— Are these my files?' He picked up one of the scrolls littering her bench.

'Duplicates,' she lied.

There had been too many for her scribes to copy, forcing Iliona to resort to the one thing that always oils wheels in the palace. Bribery.

'These are reports from the initial investigation,' he said, leafing through. 'Why are going through them again—? Ah.' He bowed. 'You see through the eyes of the blind and hear the voice of the dumb, and no, before you throw another tantrum. I am not mocking you this time. You work your oracles with trickery and mirrors. The quickness of the hand deceives the eye.'

Iliona watched an early two-tailed pasha butterfly fluttering around the arbute. Listened to the fountain splashing in the middle of the courtyard.

'Suppose,' she said, 'that the flowers are a smokescreen?'

'Like the precisely measured distance between the nooses?'

'Both suggested a ritualistic murder, but suppose that was the killer's intention?'

'Hm.' Lysander looked up at the cloudless blue sky, and seconds dragged into minutes. 'We didn't question the family of the second victims to check for alibis, therefore no leads were followed up, as we did for the general's women.'

Like a Parthian's bow, this was a long shot, Iliona thought. But suppose there was a cold-blooded killer out there, covering his tracks with a series of murders? If so, how in Hades would they pinpoint which of the six women was the original target?

* * *

Dusk was cloaking the temple precinct, softening the outlines of the treasuries, gymnasia, watercourses and statues. Up in the forests, the wolves and the porcupines would be stirring. Badgers and foxes would slink from their lairs. Down by the river, bats darted round the willows and alders. Frogs croaked from the reed beds. As the darkness deepened, Iliona watched moths dance round the flickering sconces, while the scent of rosemary and mountain thyme mingled with incense from the shrine.

'You were right.'

She jumped. One of these days, she thought, and Lysander would slit the throat of his own bloody shadow.

'His name is Tibios, and he did indeed serve the temple of Selene. Well done.'

The moon was her starting point. In the old days, long before the Olympians were born, Selene used to be worshipped in her three phases of womanhood. Developing, mature, then declining. In these enlightened days of science and mathematics, only those initiated into the priesthood even remembered this ancient wisdom — suggesting the killer was familiar with the old ways. Whether the murders were ritualistic, or whether his elaborate methods were simply a smokescreen, was irrelevant. It was a base on which to start building.

From then on, logic prevailed. The new moon was synonymous with youth, implying the intended victim was one of the daughters. But unions between citizens are contracted when the children are still in the cradle, whereas artisan women are free to wed whom they please. At sixteen, the harness-maker's daughter would have been casting around.

'With nothing else to go on,' Iliona said, 'the theory was worth testing. I'm just relieved it panned out.'

'Which is why,' Lysander said, 'my men are holding him in your office.'

Ah. 'You have insufficient enough evidence to bring him to a trial, so you're hoping I will draw a confession out of him.'

'The torture chamber is notoriously unreliable, and besides.' He shot her a sideways glance. 'I always believe in finishing what I started. Don't you?'

She made a quick calculation of what his thugs might find among her records. Surely the *Krypteia* didn't think she was foolish enough to commit incriminating evidence to paper?

'The harness-maker's daughter was called Phoebe,' he said, explaining on their way across the precinct how questioning friends and family had led to a young acolyte, who had been courting her.

'For a while, it seemed promising. Tibios is handsome enough, and he soon proved himself courteous, attentive and generous.'

The problems arose when he became too attentive. Too generous. Instead of one bottle of perfume, he would send her a dozen. It was the same with wine cakes and honeycombs. He would present her with several new bath sponges every week. And positively showered her with cheap jewels and trinkets.

'Phoebe found it overpowering, but endearing,' Lysander continued. 'It was only when Tibios began to stipulate which tunics she should wear and who she could meet with, and got angry when she refused to comply, that she realized this was not the man she wanted to marry.'

Iliona was beginning to understand. Intelligent, shrewd and obsessively tidy were the hallmarks of a controlling nature. Men like that don't take kindly to rejection.

In fact, many don't accept it, full stop.

'My lady, meet Tibios. Tibios, meet the lady who outsmarted you and secured justice for nine vulnerable women.'

Handsome, certainly. Cheekbones a tad sharp, eyes a little too narrow, but yes. She could see why Phoebe would be attracted to him. Even in shackles, he was cocky.

'I'm the one who needs justice.' The acolyte leaned so far back in the chair that its front legs were off the tiles. 'Bearing false witness is a serious crime, but that's what comes when you misinterpret entrails and cloud formations. Or was it rustling leaves and the warbling of doves?'

'You presume,' Iliona breezed, 'that you were important enough to warrant consulting the river god, but as it happens, Eurotas doesn't concern himself with parasites. You were just sloppy.'

'Sloppy?' The legs of the chair came crashing down. 'From what I've heard, the killer left nothing to chance! *Nothing!*'

As though he hadn't spoken, Iliona dripped essential oils into the burning lamps, driving out the smells of ink and dusty parchment and infusing the room with sandalwood, camphor and myrrh. Behind the chair, the guards had merged into the shadows. Leaning against the wall in the corner, Lysander could have been carved out of marble.

'That last house was barricaded from the inside,' Tibios spat. 'Tell me how getting past that isn't smart.'

'Well, now, that's exactly what I mean.' Iliona picked up an ostrich feather fan and swept it over the shelves as though it was a duster. 'You didn't need to bypass their security.'

'That's because the killer's a god. Passing through walls, or changing his shape to an insect and able to slip under doors.'

Tibios was too full of himself to question why high priestesses should be doing their own housework. Or notice that she was so unaccustomed to it, that she was using the fan upside down.

'Alas, Tibios, the truth is more mundane.' Swish-swish-swish as though he was secondary to her task. 'You were already inside.'

Another shot in the dark, although enquiries at the temple of Selene confirmed that Tibios had been off sick for the three days prior to the murder.

'You knew this family. You knew their habits and your away around, and so, having hidden yourself in their cellar, how simple to slip a tincture of poppy juice into their wine that night, and then pff! Next you're stringing them up like hams over a fire.'

'There you go again. You keep saying *me.*'

'Only because of that little stash of carvings you thought you'd hidden away. Daisies, roses and what was that other thing, captain? Lilies? Not that it matters,' she continued airily. 'Your attitude was that if you couldn't have Phoebe, nobody would, so you killed the first two families as a smokescreen—'

'Like Hades I did!' Even now, believing the lie that the captain had actually found his cache of wooden flowers, Tibios was no less arrogant. 'I wanted those bitches scared out of their skins. I wanted them to *know* they'd be next. To feel the fear in their veins and sit awake at night, worrying—and they were. Even though they'd barricaded themselves in, they couldn't sleep, couldn't eat. It wasn't just Phoebe. They ganged up against me, the whole bloody tribe, so they needed to know that you can't just toss me aside. That I had power over them, over you, over the whole bloody State.' A smug grin spread over his face. 'The smokescreen was the *fourth* family I intended to kill.'

He may have been motivated by vengeance at the beginning, but this boy enjoyed his work. He would not have stopped at four.

'Exactly how did you get that message across to these women?' Iliona laid down the fan, and now there was a contemptuous edge to her voice. 'They were unconscious when you crept out of the cellar. Unconscious when you slipped the noose round their necks, and unconscious when you hauled on the rope. That doesn't sound very powerful to me. In fact, it seems more like the hand of a coward.'

'No, no, I—'

'The trial will probably be halted for laughter, once the jury hears how this big, strong Champion of Vengeance spent three days hiding behind a sack and peeing in an olive jar.'

'It's no different from a hunter lying in wait,' he protested. 'Ouch!'

'Ooh, did that hurt?' Iliona jabbed the inside of his nostril a second time with the sharpened quill of her pen. 'That doesn't bode well, does it?' she asked the Head of the *Krypteia*. 'Remind me again what the punishment is for killing a citizen?'

'First the guilty party is paraded naked through the streets,' Lysander rumbled. 'It draws a large crowd, so of course if someone should throw something nasty at him, or take a shot with their fists, there's little my men can do to protect him.'

'That's not fair,' Tibios whined. 'I'm entitled to civility at my execution!'

'And you shall have it,' Lysander assured him. 'With great civility, you will be thrown into the Ravine of Redemption, where you can—with even more civility—contemplate your crimes as you lay bleeding.'

'That's for traitors! You can't do that to me! I'm no traitor—'

'There will be no food, no drink, no comfort down there. Just you, your broken bones, and the wolves that circle closer each day.'

'Not forgetting the moon, so white and so bright overhead,' Iliona said. 'Which will wane, and then wax again, before you eventually join the Land of the Shades.'

'Don't think you can aid your own death, either,' Lysander rumbled. 'Your hands will be tied behind your back when you're thrown. With the greatest civility, of course.'

* * *

Above the rugged peaks and fertile valleys, Night cast her web of dreams to the music of crickets and the nightingale's haunting song. Tomorrow, the countryside would ring with the drums and trumpets of the annual Corn Festival, as the first ears of wheat were offered to the goddess Demeter. How sad that the women who had worked so tirelessly to bring their crops to maturity were not here to lay their gifts on the altar.

'I suppose you were hoping it was the general behind the killings?'

The guards had long since dragged Tibios off to the dungeons, but Lysander showed no inclination to accompany them. Instead, he'd taken the chair vacated by the killer, folded his hands behind his neck and closed his eyes. It was too much for Iliona to hope he'd nodded off. Like she said before, the *Krypteia* don't sleep. Even in a cocoon of their own velvet wings.

'I can't tell you the satisfaction that clapping him in irons would have given me, after the things he wrote to the Council.' A rumble sounded in the back of his throat. It was, she realized, the first time she'd heard Lysander laugh. 'Unfortunately, as much as the general wants my job, I wasn't convinced he'd go to those lengths.'

'But you checked anyway.'

One eye opened. 'I checked.'

Iliona poured herself a goblet of dark, fruity wine. Somehow, she thought she would need it. 'What's that?' she asked, pointing to what looked like a squishy cushion wrapped in blue cotton under her desk.

'Oh, didn't I say?' The eye closed. 'It's a present.'

She drank her wine, all of it, before unwrapping the bundle. *'A hunting net?'*

'I find it quite remarkable, don't you, how so many women, who were previously considered barren, have been blessed with a much-wanted child over the last four or five years?'

Sickness rolled in the pit of her stomach.

'Spartan justice is famed throughout the world,' he continued levelly. *'Not only done, it is also seen to be done*, to quote the poet Terpander. But then.' Lysander stood up. Stretched. Rubbed the stiffness out of the back of his neck. 'Terpander was an inexhaustible composer of drinking songs, who died choking on a fig during a musical performance.'

'What are you saying?'

'I'm saying it's not a hunting net. It's a bird snare. If you look closely, you'll see the mesh is finer than the fishing net in which you currently catch your flying babies, yet strong.' He didn't even pause. 'It will dramatically reduce the time you spend on maintenance.'

'You're—not arresting me?'

'Whilst a boy with a twisted leg might not make a good warrior, Iliona, I'm sure he can weave a fine cloak or engrave a good seal.' He leaned over the desk and poured himself a goblet of wine from the bowl. 'The same way that not every man can be a cold-blooded killing machine. Some need to break free.'

Iliona's legs were so weak with relief that she had to sit down. 'Helping deserters is treachery in the eyes of the law.'

'The law can't afford to have men on the front line, who cannot be relied on.' He grinned. 'And on a more personal level, the law prefers devoting its precious time and resources to rooting out real traitors, rather than track down weaklings who will only let their country down in battle.' He refilled his goblet. 'Of course, that's only my opinion, and I would prefer you didn't bandy it around.'

Your secret's safe with me,' she said, and for heaven's sake, was she actually *laughing*?

Iliona opened the door and lifted her face to the constellations. The Lion, the Crab, and the Heavenly Twins. Far above the mulberries and vines, the paddocks and the barley fields, Night watched the High Priestess in the doorway. Guided by the stars and aided by the Fates, who measured, spun and cut the thread of life, Night had long since dried the tears of the bereaved and wrapped them in the softness of her arms. Having called on her children, Pain, Misery, Nemesis and Derision, to plague Tibios the acolyte, she was now ready to pass the baton of responsibility to her good friend, the Dawn.

And when the sun rose over the jagged peaks of Mount Parnon, some still capped with snow, Iliona smelled the scent of daisies, roses and, of course, white lilies. This time, their perfume was sweet.

Death at Delphi

Smoke, grey and nauseous, swirled round the temple. Laertes recognized bay, hemp and barley grains among the ingredients, but there were others, rich and exotic, that were foreign to him. The heat of the charcoals on which they smouldered fused with the heat of high summer.

Still breathless from the tortuous climb, Laertes bowed before the priest.

'I—'

What should he say? *I have an appointment?* It made him sound as though he was a common civil servant, not head of an army, and besides. The priest already knew why he was here. Laertes had registered his petition, paid his (truly exorbitant) fee and purified himself at the Castalian Spring, all of which was noted in the oracular records. As indeed was the gold statuette, which had propelled him to the front of the queue.

'I have sacrificed a white goat,' he told the priest. 'Its entrails—'

'Suggested favourable omens. I know.' The priest smiled as he bade him lay his armour aside. 'Come,' he said. 'Come with me, and together we will summon the spirit of Apollo, that He may answer the question you lay before Him.'

Ushered deep into the building, Laertes felt the world he knew slipping away. Gone were the crickets that rasped in the scrub. The butterflies that flittered over the cushions of wild thyme on the hillsides. Gone were the jangle of harnesses, the scrape of boots on the march. Even the sunshine was no more, for in the world of the Oracle, oil lamps flickered and strange odours danced. Music came from everywhere and nowhere. Not the music of clashing swords that Laertes was used to, nor the blare of battle trumpets. This was a soft, haunting tune made by lyres and flutes, that spoke of death, and of life, and of dreams…

From the shadows, two acolytes stepped forward in well-rehearsed unison. Boys of twelve, maybe thirteen, dressed in the same long, flowing robes as the priest.

'Drink,' the priest said, but when Laertes turned, the man was gone. In the distance, he could see small chinks of daylight. They seemed far, so far, away.

The first acolyte handed him a goblet on which the word "Forget" was engraved. The drink was wine, and Laertes drank. Then the second youth passed him a goblet on which the word "Remember" was etched. To Laertes's mind, it tasted the same. With spirals of smoke coiling round his head one second, his feet the next, they steered him towards what looked like a gaping hole in the floor. Squinting cautiously, he could see nothing but darkness below. The acolytes motioned for him to sit, then retreated in silence, taking their torches with them. Even as he'd prepared to face battle, Laertes had never known his heart beat so fast.

How long did he sit there, dangling his feet in the Stygian blackness? A minute? An hour? Time had no meaning in the world of the gods. For was this not the site where Apollo slew the dragon snake that had raped his mother when she was pregnant with him and his twin sister, Artemis? Alone in the timeless void, Laertes set to wondering for the millionth time how best to phrase his question.

Then he was falling.

Tumbling through nothingness, with his arms flailing wildly, since the smooth stone denied him a grip. Down, down he spiralled, funnelling into the blackness. In his struggle, his forehead made contact with rock, then he found flagstones cushioned with reeds. Dusting himself down, his soldier's eyes searched for the hands that had tugged at his ankles. It took only seconds to realise that his only companion was a statue of Apollo—

'Welcome,' a voice echoed. It was thin and crackled with age. 'Welcome to the world of answers and truth.'

Making the sign of the horns, Laertes traced the sound to a narrowed entrance over which "None may enter" was written in gold lettering. From the doorway, he peered into a small inner sanctum lit by the dim flame from a tripod. Its flickering light revealed a solitary female, veiled and seated upon a stool.

'Welcome to the point where heaven and earth and east and west meet. The navel of the world, that is home to the Oracle.'

What had he been expecting? An old woman, to be sure. Wisdom went hand in hand with age and prophesy, and he remembered now that the previous sibyl's trance had turned her into a wild animal, thrashing and groaning as she frothed on the floor, to die only a few hours later. Would that happen now? Listening to drumbeats and doves cooing curiously close by, Laertes was transfixed by the frail figure bent over her tripod, still dressed in the wedding robes of her marriage long ago to long-haired Apollo. To his shame, his strong limbs were trembling.

'Dost thou wish to enquire of the Lord of Light and Prophesy, whose arrows of knowledge shine into the future?' she quavered.

'I do.'

'Art thou pure of body and heart?'

'I am.'

'Then Apollo will speak to thee through the vessel of my body. What is it thou wishes to know?'

'My question…' He cleared his throat. He was a general, after all. A commander of men. 'My question is this.'

His mouth was dry. Was it the smoke, the vile smell, or the fact that this was the first time he had voiced his intentions so bluntly?

'The king who rules the city-state from which I come is a weak man. He puts the good of himself before the good of his people, and I want to know if … if …' The words did not come easily. '… I move to unseat him—'

'Whether thy campaign will succeed?'

He didn't feel better, now it was out in the open. His heart still pounded harder than a blacksmith's hammer on the anvil. 'Yes,' he said eventually.

'Then shall ye know.'

With a twirl of her wrist, an explosion erupted from the tripod, a flurry of sparks flew into the air, then she hugged her arms tight to her chest and began rocking back and forth, keening softly. Swaying himself in the abominable heat of this underground tomb, Laertes watched the flames from her fire reflect in the Pool of Prophesy at her feet and sensed the past and the future fusing together. It wasn't only the crack on his head, he thought, that was making it throb.

Time passed. The Oracle rocked, wailed, muttered and reeled. The flames in her tripod guttered and died. In their place, smoke, white and sweet, welled from the walls, from the floor, from the ceiling. Laertes' tunic clung, sodden, against his skin.

'When a guest of wood doth pass through thy portals.' When she spoke, it was in a voice unrecognisable from the tremulous warble of old age. This voice was low, deep and even. 'Then must thou build a city of metal walls and woollen roofs, and set it beside the dancing pebbles.'

The sweat on his back turned inexplicably cold.

'Sacrifice in this place a creature that makes both music and food, and I, Apollo of the Lyre, will surely march at thy side.'

With a jerk, she slumped forward. The drumbeats fell silent. The cooing of doves ceased at once.

'Leave me,' the old woman quavered, and her voice was so weak he had to strain to hear it. 'Leave me, for I am spent.'

Perhaps he should have thanked her, but she seemed barely conscious, so he turned, and the last sight was of her thin breast rising and falling with unnatural rapidity. He did not understand the riddle, but, as he clambered up the rope ladder that had been lowered through the hole, he knew there was a priest in the temple, a seer called Periander, who would help him unravel the mystery. With the seer's help, and with Apollo's, there was no doubt in his mind that his revolt would succeed.

Tumbling back into the real world, Laertes was positively breathless with relief.

* * *

Below, in the underground sanctum, the Oracle threw off the veil that filtered the fumes and stretched her slender arms high.

'How many more?' she asked the wall.

The wall parted, spilling a thin finger of light into the cavern. 'Five,' the young man said, consulting his scroll by the glow of his candle. 'Though none of the other petitioners require such elaborate theatre.'

'Good. I was half-choked with that smoke.'

'You were?' The young man laid his drums aside and squeezed through the gap in the false wall. 'When you tossed those herbs into the tripod and set off that explosion, I had to pinch my nose to stop myself sneezing.'

Cassandra smiled with him. 'Next time, I'll stow a smaller bunch of borage up my sleeve, but at least Laertes should have no trouble interpreting the riddle.' She pulled off her old woman's mask and blotted the sweat off her face with her sleeve. 'I made it simple enough, I thought.'

When a guest of wood doth pass through thy portals—in other words, when a ship enters harbour—that's the time to *build a city of metal walls and woollen roofs*—i.e. set up camp, since soldiers use spears to support their blankets. And if this didn't make it plain that this undertaking should be conducted in the spring, when the seas opened once more for trade, *beside the dancing pebbles,* she had added firmly. It wouldn't take much working out on Laertes' part that this meant when the first snowmelts cascade down the mountains, and as for sacrificing *a creature that makes both music and food*—well, what other animal's flesh is succulent when roasted and whose shell makes the perfect soundbox for a lyre, other than a tortoise?

'Laertes is a soldier, not a politician, my love.' Jason began to knead the muscles in her neck that tightened from hours bent over the tripod. 'Men like him think in straight lines. Not too rough?'

'No, that's lovely,' she purred.

'I'll bet you a chalkoi to an obol that Laertes heads straight for Periander.' He moved down to massage the knots in her shoulders. 'He's the very sort who needs a seer to solve the puzzle for him — and ho, ho, talk of the devil.'

An older man in ankle-length robes, whose craggy face was softened by a beard, shinned down the ladder with the skill of a ship's rat.

'Father!' Cassandra embraced him warmly. 'What a delightful surprise!'

She hadn't seen much of him over the past six months, and he had never, in her recollection, come down here to see her. Was this because she was too engrossed in her new appointment, she wondered? Or because the memories that this sanctum held were too painful for him?

'Did you solve the riddle for our rebellious general? Because all in all, I thought it went rather well,' she decided.

The admission fee, the costs of purification, one gold statuette, plus what? a silver wine cup, perhaps, for the seer's deciphering. Traitor or not, the Delphic Treasury would welcome Laertes back any time.

'I suppose, Cassandra, that depends how one defines the word "well".' Periander's eyes were grave, but then they always were. 'Laertes collapsed at my feet.'

'And?' she cried.

'And he's dead,' her father said quietly.

* * *

Ever so softly, Night threw her cloak over the mount of Parnassus. Flexing the stiffness out of her legs, Cassandra paced the portico as, one by one, the priests and attendants made their way home to their wives and their supper and bed. The last of the petitioners was long gone, the temple swept with purifying hyssop in readiness for tomorrow, and the only sound that broke the silence was the grinding of bolts, as the sanctuary was locked up against thieves. She paced and paced until only the creatures of darkness prowled the Sacred Way that zigzagged its way up to the shrine. Fox, jackal, hedgehog and caracal. They moved from shadow to shadow.

Dead? How could Laertes be dead?

In the Pool of Purification, she saw a young woman with hair blacker than a raven's wing and eyes darker than an adulterous liaison. Plunging her hands into the cool, clear water, Cassandra splashed her face with her own reflection.

With the temple physician laid up in splints after a fall, there was no one to confirm or refute the cursory diagnosis that cause of death was a weak heart. Several witnesses testified to the chills and sweats that Laertes experienced beforehand, but then most supplicants suffered similar effects at the prospect of coming face to face with the gods. As for being breathless after his consultation, there was nothing unusual about that, either. The higher a petitioner's status, the harder the temple worked at disorientating him, because farmers, for instance, eager to know the most auspicious time to plant their beans or bring in their harvest, were far less worldly than kings or insurgent generals. Deeply religious, highly superstitious, the peasant folk believed with all their hearts that Apollo's spirit spoke to them straight through the mouth of the Oracle. They didn't need further convincing.

But a crown is not held in place by thin air. Kingship requires plotting and scheming, travel and trade, just as it requires war and diplomacy. Such sophisticates are not easily fooled and are even less likely to trust. Hence, the magic that is brought into play.

Senses manipulated by darkness, by narcotic fumes, by strange haunting music. Rituals take on even greater importance. The petitioners are passed from one priest to another before they are able to take stock of their surroundings. They're given goblets of wine that will supposedly make them forget everything except the focus of their question yet remember clearly the Oracle's prediction. Then they are left alone to commune with the gods, and who would imagine that an old woman's hands could grip their ankles and drag them into the void?

Disorientated by their fall every bit as much as the blackness, they do not see the old woman hurry back to her stool. But—! (And it was always possible). One of these days, this chicanery might just bounce off their defences. In which case, keeping the petitioner outside the inner sanctum, where there was no possibility of him seeing that the face was a mask, was essential.

As indeed was the Oracle's constant monitoring of the supplicant's body language and expression from beneath her veil…

High overhead, Hercules wielded his olive-wood club and the moon rose full and white through the pines. Cassandra sat on the steps of the temple and buried her head in her hands. Weak heart be damned. While she was teasing Laertes with her riddles, what she had mistaken for nervousness and disorientation were, in fact, the symptoms of a man who was dying. Dying in front of her eyes.

And manifesting all the symptoms of poison.

* * *

'Jason.' She had to shake him twice to rouse him. 'Jason, wake up.'

When he saw her, fully dressed and her hair still pinned up, he was on his feet in an instant. 'What's wrong?'

'Laertes was murdered,' she explained, while he pulled on a tunic. In the lamplight, his skin shone like bronze. 'I need you to go down to the temple mortuary.'

She did not need to elaborate. Women, even the most important woman in Delphi, were forbidden to set foot inside.

'Examine his body, check his eyes, his skin colour, look in his mouth, his ears, under his nails, then report back to me on your findings.'

She was pretty certain she knew what had killed him, having ruled out corn cockle, since Laertes had suffered no abdominal cramps, while aconite would have had him throwing up, and with hellebore he'd have been salivating like a rabid dog. Other poisons were either too slow or too fast and so, given the timescale in which he died, Cassandra concluded that only belladonna could have taken his life. But confirmation would not go amiss.

'I love you, I adore you, I would give my life for you,' Jason said, combing his tousled hair with his hands. 'But frankly, my darling, I'd rather face the Minotaur in Hades than ask the Keepers of the Vigil to stand aside while I poke and prod their dead charge at this ungodly hour of the night. What excuse am I supposed to give them?'

'I have absolutely no idea,' she said, smiling in spite of herself. 'But you did so well today, with the drumbeats and doves, that I'm sure you'll come up with something.'

The invisible doves of prophesy were Cassandra's idea, but the drums and the white smoke had been Jason's. All it needed, he'd insisted, was a bowl of hot water and some terracotta pipes to filter the steam. Delphi, after all, was founded on the principle that the quickness of the hand deceives the eye.

'Ah, the birds.' He clucked his tongue. 'I wasn't sure it would work,' he admitted. 'I feared blocking the light from my one tiny flame would make no difference when I threw the sheet over their cage, but bless you, my love, you were right. They stopped talking at once.'

'I wish you would,' she said. 'We have so little time.'

'Why the hurry?'

She pressed her lover's hand in urgency. 'I'll explain later,' she said. There wasn't time now to go into why she needed to unmask Laertes' killer during her first trance of the morning.

'For you, O Prophetic One.' He kissed her lightly on the nose. 'I will borrow Hermes' winged sandals and fly like Pegasus himself.'

Watching him sprint across the courtyard, she thought it wouldn't be the first time that the Oracle had delivered a prophesy, only for it not to come true. Accuracy wasn't essential. Had Laertes died trying to overthrow his sovereign, it would only prove that, although Apollo had been with him, Zeus or Poseidon had sided with his opponent. When it comes to gods battling it out, no one argues.

In addition, many riddles were deliberately open to misinterpretation. Some for political reasons. Some because bribes had been passed (the Treasury was no slouch when it came to filling its storehouses). And some because, quite simply, Cassandra had no idea how to answer. Thanks to the meticulously maintained library of files at Delphi, she knew who the supplicants were, where they came from, the political background. But there was never any advance notice of their question.

And today the Oracle had quite clearly foretold that Laertes would set up camp beside the river next spring.

The Oracle could not afford to be that wrong.

Outside, Selene's silver light spilled over the rooftops, bathing the theatre, the shrines, the fountains in silver as bats squeaked on the wing. With a thousand city states constantly at war with one another, Delphi remained spectacularly neutral. In fact, it thrived on optimism, Cassandra decided, as she waited for Jason to return. And it was her job to keep it that way. Without optimism, one tiny shrine could not have grown into the most prestigious religious centre in the world, bursting with treasuries, overflowing with marble, and where eight hundred statues stared out to sea. Thanks to its oracles, a federation of small (and otherwise insignificant) city states had grown to become the most powerful council in the Greek world. Today, it was not so much a case of consulting the Oracle as obtaining sanction. Kings would not make war without it.

But Cassandra was only one link in the chain and, incredible as it may seem, not even the most important.

If anything happened to her—and the sibyls had a curious habit of dying in agony—there were other girls trained to step into her bridal robes and take that famous seat over the tripod. Girls like her cousin Hermione, for example, who'd been primed to take over, had it not been for Cassandra's outstanding aptitude for deception. She smiled in recollection. The Governing Council, always eager to stock a new treasury, revelled in the fact that each new generation brought fresh ideas to the role. Cassandra's proposal to enclose her lover, Jason, behind a partition to add to the drama cast poor Hermione into oblivion.

'Great Zeus, what are you doing out alone this time of night?'

She spun round. 'Father! You frightened the life out of me!'

Grey eyes stared solemnly at her in the moonlight. She tried to remember the last time he'd smiled, but could not. 'Can't you sleep, child?'

'Can't you?' she retorted. Like her, he was still in his day robes.

'The death of those carried young to the Elysian Fields is tragedy beyond measure,' he said sadly. 'To have them die before one's eyes is a burden greater than Atlas, who holds the whole world on his shoulders.'

Periander wrapped one arm round her shoulder and squeezed. Together father and daughter watched the moon dance on the sea.

'We old folk find consolation in the knowledge and wisdom that comes from maturity, but it is always the young that we envy, Cassandra.' He sighed heavily. 'You have so much to give.' He placed a kiss on the top of her head. 'So much to lose.'

She watched him walk away, stroking his beard in thought, though it was only later, much later, that she realised he wasn't talking about a young general collapsing dead at his feet.

He had been talking about Cassandra's mother.

* * *

What befell Periander's wife befell most of the Delphic prophetesses. One day the Oracle was sitting in her sanctum, dispensing riddles as usual. The next, she was a gibbering wreck. Drooling, moaning, writhing, screaming. She saw visions—terrible, marvellous, hideous visions—but these were the visions that killed her. Slowly and painfully, they would torture her to death while she frothed at the mouth, suffered spasms, amnesia, until the final convulsion came as a blessing.

Cassandra was just a baby when her mother had died. She only ever knew her through her father's memories, but, from what he told her, she would have loved her. They shared the same dark hair and eyes, he said, the same sense of joy and laughter.

'Ah, but she was a wonderful actress,' Periander would remind her. 'The minute she donned those robes and mask, she became Apollo's virgin bride, waiting for her adoring bridegroom.'

Then he would explain how it wasn't that the Oracle was a fraud. Just that Mighty Apollo couldn't sit there, day in and day out, with nothing else to do but assure this merchant that his investment was sound or that poet that his next work would be a masterpiece. When the gods spoke, mortals knew it, Periander reminded her solemnly, and when Apollo *did* speak through the mouth of the Oracle, then the poor creature was doomed. But by maintaining the pretence, such was Delphi's standing in the Greek world that men came from all over to receive the god's approbation, undergoing various rituals to win Him over. It was vital their trust in Him was upheld.

Backed by a massive administration ranging from the Governing Council to the countless scribes that toiled to keep the mountain of files up to date, the Oracle hosted Games to rival Olympia and held musical competitions that would turn Orpheus himself green with envy. And thus, for the thousands of pilgrims who flocked to the shrine hoping to have a curse lifted or find love, found a new colony overseas or sue for peace with their neighbours, the Oracle represented stability in a changing and unsettled world.

'You, child, are even better than your mother,' Periander would tell her, and for her part, Cassandra was proud to contribute to the miracle that was Delphi. Rich or poor, every petitioner went home reassured that, if he sacrificed here or did penance there, Apollo would surely be with him. The emancipation of slaves was particularly rewarding for her. You couldn't ask for more than to give a man happiness.

And so, watching her father prostrate himself before the shrine of Zeus, the moonlight turning the lines in his face into chasms, her heart ached for the man whose wife had died after hearing Apollo's voice, and who had never got over the loss. And now, to add to the tragedy, his daughter's prophesies had been brutally sabotaged…

As he rose and poured a libation to the King of the Immortals, God of Vengeance and Justice and Honour, she realised with a start that her mother would have been the same age Cassandra was now. In her twenty-fifth summer.

Despite the throbbing heat of the night, the Oracle shivered. And wished Jason would hurry.

* * *

Zeus is the first, Zeus is the last, Zeus is the god with the divine thunderbolt.

The hymn kept going round in her mind.

Zeus is the head, Zeus is the middle, of Zeus all things have their end.

As she gazed down over the hillside, across the building works in various stages of construction, at the statues that lined the Sacred Way, Cassandra knew that she would remember this night for the rest of her life.

It was the night she walked into womanhood.

Behind her, the Shining Cliffs lived up to their name, glistening white in the moonlight. Riddled with caves and rich with fountains and springs, they were the playground of Pan, home to the Muses, and the stairway to the pinnacle from which those convicted of sacrilege against the gods were flung to their deaths. From the grove of holm oaks, an owl hooted softly.

Not a seer like her father, or a prophetess as was made out, Cassandra nevertheless saw the picture clear in her mind.

The king who rules the city-state from which I come is a weak man. Laertes' words floated back to her. *He puts the good of himself before the good of his people.*

The files had backed up this assessment, but weak and self-serving doesn't mean stupid. One by one, as Hercules tramped round the heavens, the pieces fell into place.

Laertes' king hadn't trusted his general an inch, and when Laertes set off on that long trek to Delphi, the king knew there could be only one question which needed an answer. Not about to give up his dynasty, he duly despatched his own man, an assassin, to ensure Laertes would not return.

Leaning her back against a pillar, Cassandra realised she'd never know for certain. Had the assassin travelled a different route, which took longer? Had he been caught in a storm out at sea? Taken ill? Who knows, but whatever happened, he must have arrived in Delphi well after Laertes had registered his petition and paid his admission fee. Prowling round on padded feet, enquiring in whispers, the assassin would have noted the power that one gold statuette held, shooting Laertes up the queue of merchants and military men, athletes and musicians, much less the scores of humble smallholders. And the assassin would have quickly realised that, if the Treasury could be bought, so could individuals. It was his nature to probe and investigate. To determine which priest drank from gold goblets at home. Which acolyte kept an expensive mistress. Whether the Guardian of the Keys had run up debts.

From the moment Laertes set foot outside his own country, he was a dead man. It had only been a question of timing. Cassandra understood. This was the way of the world. It was the next part she had trouble comprehending. The fact that the murder had not only happened in *her* world, but that the killer specifically intended to discredit the Oracle.

And she did not mean the assassin.

His job was over once he'd established who could be bribed, and how much. Even the method of execution was out of his hands.

Poison…

Extracted from the deadly nightshade, its juice induces dry mouth, impaired speech — all the things, in fact, that she had witnessed from inside her sanctum before Laertes' eyesight failed and he'd find difficulty breathing, prior to lapsing into unconsciousness and finally death. The heat from the column diffused into her backbone. It all came back to that tiny phial of liquid that had been fed to him inside the temple, she reflected, and that was the sad part. *Inside* the temple. For in this killing, timing was crucial. And, standing beneath the stars and the moon that saw everything, Cassandra knew that the hand that had delivered that fatal dose of belladonna belonged to someone not only familiar with the temple, but who knew the sanctum inside out. Who understood not only the mind of the petitioner, but also the intricacies of the disorientation process—and was in a position to play on both. Manipulating the timing of the drug, so that Laertes wouldn't notice anything out of the ordinary, whilst ensuring that the Oracle's suspicions would not be aroused, either. Someone, in short, who knew she would set the supplicant a riddle. And be discredited when Laertes collapsed of natural causes…

It was not coincidence, she realised with a chill, that the temple physician was laid up with a broken leg. His fall from the Shining Cliffs was a nudge, not a stumble, and her stomach churned as she remembered who it was, who'd raced down the cliffs to sound the alarm—

'So that's where you're hiding!'

His voice broke the silence now, and as she turned, Cassandra's limbs were shaking.

Ah, but she was a wonderful actress, her father said of her mother. *But you. You are even better.*

This was true. Her smile was wide as she greeted him brightly.

'Jason!' She injected relief into her voice. 'I thought you'd gone back to bed! So now tell me. What symptoms did you find on Laertes' body?'

'That's what took me so long,' he said, and when he moved towards her, she backed away. 'No matter how hard I pleaded, no matter what tricks I pulled, the Guardians of the Vigil would not let me near him.'

Cassandra wished she could have sounded surprised.

* * *

In the darkness of the inner sanctum, music that was a combination of Persian and Egyptian, Phoenician and Arabic filtered down from the temple. Behind the partition painted to resemble the rock face, the doves of prophesy cooed, and in the tripod, sweet-smelling herbs emitted their scents. Lemon balm, oregano and mint.

She was a wonderful actress, but you, child, you are better.

In the past, whenever a sibyl had heard the true voice of Apollo, she had complained of smoke rising from a fissure in the floor that gave off a light, scented odour. The breath of the god. After which she fell into that fateful, delirious trance—

Wailing and thrashing in her created odour, Cassandra's actions quickly attracted the attention of the priests and acolytes above. Jason burst through the false wall in alarm.

'What is it, my love? What's the matter?'

When she didn't respond, he called for 'Water! Light! Give her air!' And when he tried to lift her off the stool, he found that he could not. A crowd gathered round, her father among them, his face a picture of agony.

I'm sorry, so sorry, she wanted to tell him. *I know this is how you found my mother so long ago, but truly I know no other way...*

The Oracle could not — must not — be discredited.

Even at the expense of her own father's pain.

Soon the Council came running, the heavyweights who ran the administration, and the aristocrats who governed it. Through her twitching and groaning, Cassandra saw the face of her cousin, Hermione, at the edge of the crush. Familial concern tinged with more than just a little hopefulness, she noticed through her jibbering. Poor, sweet Hermione. Fated to be disappointed again.

'I see death which is not a death,' she howled, and there was no need to disguise her voice. This was Apollo speaking through Cassandra's own voice, just as he had through previous sibyls'.

'Laertes,' someone hissed in translation. 'She means it was murder.'

Her arms flailed. 'From fruit which is not a fruit.'

'Poison,' whispered somebody else.

'I see the shadow of the Ferryman inside this chamber.'

Beside her, Jason's frame had gone unaccountably still and, as her frenzy caused her to toss more herbs of prophesy into the eternal flame, she reflected again on how handsome he was. How funny. How virile. *How cunning.*

'Who?' one of the priests asked. 'Who killed Laertes?'

But the Oracle was passing into convulsions, and as she thrashed, Cassandra noticed her father slip away from the sanctum, tears streaming down his bearded cheeks. She ached to go with him, hug him tight to her breast, show him that his daughter was not dying. But the Oracle could not leave. Rooted to her stool—to her destiny—Cassandra tore at her hair in grief and despair.

You are better than your mother…

She was not, she was not, this anguish was real. Here, before the Governing Council and the enterprise that was Delphi, she was betraying the only man she'd ever loved.

'Can you see in your flames the face of the murderer?' one of the Elders asked. 'Do you see the face of the man who sought to bring disgrace on this place?'

Not in the flames, she wanted to scream. I see his face here, in my heart.

'Zeus is the foundation of the earth and the sky.' She was supposed to be rambling. She might as well ramble from the hymn that had kept her awake all through the night. And the images that had tormented her with it. 'Zeus is the breath of all things.'

'She means divine retribution will befall him,' someone interpreted.

'I see two heads in a womb and two quivers of arrows. And the bear will ride on the back of the dolphin and smite the beast that tried to kill him.'

'Twins!' an acolyte shouted. 'She means twins,' and suddenly all the priests were chorusing at once.

'The dolphin is Apollo—'

'—his arrows are rays of light!'

It must be the shock of the Oracle's trance, she decided. Otherwise they'd have realised instantly that the dolphin was Apollo's sacred emblem, just as the bear was his sister's.

'Apollo is telling us that sacrilege has been perpetrated against him, but that Artemis, the huntress will strike down the assassin on behalf of her brother.'

Mutterings ran round the sanctum.

'The killer has already left Delphi—'

'—but we need take no action ourselves—'

'—because Apollo will have his revenge through his sister!'

'Justice is served,' someone pronounced.

But what was justice, if not a matter of perspective? From the corner of her eye, she glanced at Jason. His face might as well have been carved of stone. Tasked with ensuring Laertes' death, the assassin had been true to his mission, and in so doing he had saved a crown and a dynasty. To his king, crushing rebellion was righteous. The assassin would be a hero when he returned — but what justice for the man who fed Laertes the poison?

With a final shriek, Cassandra threw her arms into the air then collapsed onto the floor. This was the sign that the Oracle had stopped prophesying. Visions were only possible when seated upon her sacred stool. The crowd gasped.

'It's a miracle!'

'The trance hasn't claimed her life after all.'

Even Hermione appeared relieved.

'Apollo has spoken without killing his mouthpiece — '

'— he wants us to know that this sacrilege will be avenged.'

As they trickled out, the Council, the priests, even Jason, who she noticed was shaking, four words echoed inside her head. *Sacrilege will be avenged.* Yes, it would, she thought dully. Sacrilege would be avenged, but not in the way they imagined.

Only she, Cassandra, had the power to do that …

Alone in her sanctum, the Oracle wept.

* * *

'I'm so sorry, Cassandra.' The priests bade the stretcher bearers lay down their burden. 'You have our deepest sympathy.'

The body was covered by linen, but the red stains told their own story. She stared with a heart that was broken.

'It was the will of the gods, Cassandra. Apollo needed a sacrifice, and since he spared your life, he took the life of someone you loved.'

Not Apollo, she thought heavily. He took his own life…

'We found him lying at the foot of the pinnacle.' The priests shuffled awkwardly. 'There was … nothing anybody could do.'

Knowing sympathy was inadequate, they retreated, leaving her alone with the body. How long, though, an hour? before they trooped back? Not long, that's for sure, since it was essential that the obsequies commenced as quickly as possible, and since women were not allowed inside the temple mortuary, this was her only—and last—time alone with him. She wished she could make peace with him, too.

We named you Cassandra, your mother and I, because during the time of the Trojan War, Cassandra's curse was to prophesy but not be believed. Her father's words echoed in the stillness. *We thought, no we* <u>*hoped*</u>*, it would spare you the fate of the previous sibyls. But you, child—*he had smiled—*you were always so headstrong.*

'The name Jason means healing,' a voice rasped at her shoulder. 'Which I will, if you will allow me.'

She looked up at him, blond and bronzed, and thought her heart would break in two. He knew. He knew the minute he'd tried to inspect Laertes' corpse that something wasn't right…

'I prised it out of the Keepers of the Vigil in the end,' he had told her. 'If no one was allowed near the body, then only someone in authority could have issued that command. I made them divulge who, then I knocked up the temple physician.'

That's why he was gone so long, he explained.

'The physician said that Periander had been acting oddly for a few days, and that he'd been worried.'

It was why the physician agreed to go for a walk above the Shining Cliffs with him, and why he'd accepted it had been Periander's clumsiness, not malice, that had caused him to fall and break his ankle.

Jason stared at the blooded sheet on the bier stained by one tear, then another, then another. 'Your father was not a bad man,' he whispered.

'With so many choices open to him, so many different paths he could have taken,' she sobbed, 'why did he choose to become a cold-blooded killer?'

'Because, darling, he loved you.'

Anger replaced grief. 'It was not for him to decide Laertes' fate,' Cassandra spat. 'Between us we could have used the oracle to divert Laertes from his murderous intentions, or at least warn him of the assassin at his back. After that, it would be up to him how he proceeded, not for my father to decide.'

Jason watched her tears darken the shroud.

'Laertes came to Delphi to receive sanction for the rebellion he was planning. The king's assassin followed,' he said. 'By listening and observing, he found a willing implement in, yes, this temple's seer of all people, but don't be too harsh on your father, my love. We all have something we want desperately, and we all have something to trade. Your father simply wanted to save his daughter's life.'

Old sequences replayed in her head. Periander grief-stricken when his beloved wife fell ill to the noxious vapours inside the sanctum. But not half so pained as the day his only child announced that she was following the same career path as her mother.

'To spare you the agony of dying young, your father became the assassin's instrument, feeding Laertes belladonna in the belief that, whatever happened, Laertes was a dead man, but this way he could at least save his daughter.'

If only it were that simple, Cassandra thought. He argued that, if he discredited the oracle and another prophetess took her place, what did principle matter, provided his daughter was safe? But did he not realise? That she not only understood but accepted, when she donned the bridal robes, that the deadly vapours that rose from the rock would probably kill her. But weighed against the balance of life, the opportunity to become the holy Oracle at Delphi was the most exciting, the most challenging, the most invigorating role any woman could hope to take on.

'To live a few years fully is better than to live many years badly,' she said, hugging her arms to her breast.

Once again, the decision was not her father's to make, but the tragedy was, with Jason's assistance, she had arranged that circus this morning specifically to convince Periander that his daughter had breathed the vapours of death and that there was nothing for him to live for. Sacrilege in Apollo's shrine had indeed been punished. But at what price, she wondered—

'Come,' Jason said. 'The priests are returning. Let's go back to the sanctum.' He kissed her cheek-stained tears. 'There's a fissure I want to block up.'

Healing, he said. The name Jason means healing and maybe, just maybe, Cassandra would grow to love him as much as he adored her.

Right now, though, she doubted it.

How could she love him, if she hated herself?

Desperate House Wines

Benjamin Hardcastle didn't know much about women. If he had, he wouldn't have invited his wife, his girlfriend and his estranged daughter to spend the weekend in an obscure vineyard in the south west of France. Leastways, not all at the same time.

He might also have warned them that this wasn't any old obsure vineyard in the south west of France. It was his. He'd bought it with the proceeds of his lottery win, and wanted them to share his excitement.

Unfortunately, investments was another flair outside Benjamin Hardcastle's sphere of expertise. As a small, independent supplier of wines to local restaurants, there was a reason why *Le Château d'Aphrodite* was going cheap. Ravaged by the COVID crisis, when restaurants closed for months, putting many out of business in the process, the vineyard was in deep, dark, dire financial straits. And it didn't help that the closest thing Benjamin knew about wine-making was how to open a bottle.

As it happened, Gabriel Larroque didn't know much about women, either. He was a wine-maker by trade, and a damned good one at that. Which wasn't why he'd been hired to manage the vineyard. A long-distance lorry driver by trade, Benjamin didn't know his *bonjour* from his *merci*, and desperately needed someone whose English was perfect. Happily for him, Gabriel turned out to be much more than a bilingual expert. He was a good listener, which is what Benjamin needed more than anything else. Until the day he was found dead in his own cellar, and zat was not ze only *problème*. Monsieur Ardcassle was very much alive at 8pm. Not so an hour later—and this was where things got tricky.

Death was hardly accidental, and it most certainly wasn't suicide.

Benjamin Hardcastle was found tied to a chair, with half a ton of clingfilm wrapped round his face.

Which is where things got even trickier. The doors to the outside were locked, only four people had a key, and CCTV showed that no one had entered or left the estate. In other words, all four key-holders were inside *Le Château d'Aphrodite* that night, and Gabriel could have sworn that the three women were with him the entire time that Benjamin was missing.

* * *

'Poppycock.' The wife, technically the widow, spiked her hands through her hair. 'The idea that it was one of us is balderdash.'

Sometimes, Gabriel thought that English people invented words simply to annoy foreigners.

'It's perfectly obvious that someone resented the take-over, broke in and took their revenge. My money's on the previous owner.'

'That would be difficult, Madame Ardcassle—'

'Faye. Please. Since we're effectively under house arrest until those idiot police find the real culprit, the least you can do is call me Faye.'

'Of course. Faye.' She was a fine-looking woman. Not an ounce of fat, either, despite teetering on forty, and would be even more handsome if she ditched that unflattering blonde bob that British women seem addicted to. 'But it is 'ard to see how the former proprietor could have killed your 'usband, when zey buried 'im last spring.'

'Ex-husband! Do you know how long we'd been separated? Five and a half years, and *still* the bastard wouldn't sign the divorce papers. I mean, seriously! How long can you stay angry with someone?'

'He wasn't angry, 'e was hurt.'

Two days had passed since the swarm of police, technicians and forensics crews had vacated the premises, and quite frankly if a hurricane had swept through, it would have left less of a mess. Gabriel had only gone down to the cellar once since then, summoning every ounce of courage to face the spot where his employer's life had been sucked so viciously from him, and he wasn't ashamed to admit that his hand was shaking as he'd eased open the door. In the four months that he'd worked here, their bond of friendship had grown stronger by the day, and the idea that someone—anyone—could do such a wicked thing was sickening beyond belief. Especially in this dark, dusty, silent sanctuary, where bottles lay undisturbed for years except by the spiders, and was almost spiritual in its solitude.

'I understand that. I do.'

They were in the office, which looked like it had been ransacked by a pack of naughty children. Gabriel trying to sort the paperwork, Faye rolling up the cables, after the police had taken away Benjamin's laptop, phone and tablet, without bothering to unplug them from the wall.

'Thing is, I'd been living a lie for so long, and when he talked about starting a family, I couldn't pretend any more. Obviously, it hurt him. Me coming out like that. And maybe I could have handled it better at the time. But five and a half years is way too long to hold a grudge.'

''E didn't resent you being gay.' *She broke my heart, Gabe.* 'He was 'urt because you didn't confide in 'im, and the marriage was a sham—'

'Sham?' Faye scrubbed at a patch of graphite stains that Gabriel knew from experience, when the police dusted for fingerprints after his parents had been burgled, were never going to shift with soap and water. 'He's the one who shacked up with the first little bitch to bat her fake eyelashes at him. How do you think that made me feel?' She waved her soggy sponge with menace. 'Supplanted by the sort that, if a burglar broke in and stole the TV, she'd run after him and say *here, you forgot the remote*. God knows what he saw in her.'

Attraction of opposites would be Gabriel's guess. Brunette, where Faye was blonde. Bubbly, where Faye was serious. A hands-on hairdresser, where Faye worked in an office.

'If it's any consolation, Benjamin didn't like your new life partner, either. Felt she was…what is the word? Sponging off you. Zat you were living in a nice, big 'ouse with a good job in sales, paying all ze bills, when she contributed nothing.'

'Bianca's a street artiste. There's no money in her line of work, and don't forget. If he'd signed those bloody papers, half the proceeds from the house—which is just an end-of-terrace, by the way—would have been his.'

Calls herself the finest living statue south of London, but truth is, Gabe, the only reason she stands still all day is coz she's too bleedin' lazy to get a job.

'That was pure spite on his part, saying all Bianca did was take, take, take. From the outset, he was hell-bent on undermining our relationship. Couldn't accept that I was happy, and belittling my partner was his way of punishing me. Sod it.' Faye opened the office window and threw the sponge as far and as hard as she could. 'I've had enough of cleaning, I've had enough of Benjamin, I've had enough of the whole damn bloody lot.'

The door would have rattled on its hinges, had it not been made of oak. Gabriel turned towards the window. The police were convinced that hate was the motive for the murder, and since all three women nurtured it with passion, it was simply a question of deciding which one was the killer.

The wife? On the grounds that her husband wouldn't give her what she wanted, namely a divorce, then brought her across to rub her nose in it.

The girlfriend, Melodie? Not because she and the victim had split up several months ago— funnily enough, just around the time Hardcastle won several million on the lottery, and the first she found out about the win was here. But where she was looking forward to a romantic reconciliation, she arrived to find that she was expected to share him with two other women, including that bitch of an ex.

And then there was the daughter. Chloe. The girl whose mother Benjamin dumped the second he found out that she was pregnant. For twenty-four-years, Chloe had no idea who her father was, until a letter landed on her doormat, telling her that she'd won a weekend in France, all expenses paid. At which point Benjamin dropped his paternal bombshell, somehow expecting this bright, spunky stranger to welcome him with open arms.

Gabriel couldn't fault the reasoning. Betrayal is a powerful motive, and hell hath no fury like a woman scorned, but—

'OK. What was Faytal Attraction saying about me this time?'

Melodie's voice made him jump. He hadn't heard her come in.

'That I'm the sort who tiptoes round the house, so as not to wake the sleeping pills?'

Despite the situation, Gabriel smiled. 'Something like zat.'

'You know she was the reason Beni and me split up?'

She didn't give him chance to answer.

'Long-distance lorry drivers are hardly ever home, but when he was it was *can you fix the washer on the tap? The fence post's broken. The hinge on the kitchen cupboard snapped...* But what really got me was, he never said get a plumber, hire an electrician, look it up on YouTube and fix it yourself, you useless cow.'

You have to remember, it was still my house, Gabe. I had responsibilities—

'He spoke very 'ighly of your DIY skills.'

'Damn right. The salon would be running at a loss, if I called in a professional every time a bulb popped or the u-bends clogged.'

Big, brown eyes filled with tears. From grief, at losing the only man she ever loved? Regret, for what could have been? Or were they tears of conscience?

'I thought Beni was The One, I really did, but the way he jumped every time Faytal Attraction snapped her fingers—? He spent more time at hers than he did at mine, and that's why I wouldn't take him back. At no stage, not once, did he promise to stop going round, then out of the blue I got this.'

She showed Gabriel the text.

Whatever it takes to make us work, I'll do it, babes, and that's a promise.

'Ever since we split up, he'd been bombarding me with emails, texts and calls, swearing on his mother's grave how much he loved me, how he'd make it up to me, but I never believed him until he sent this.'

Remember that big house in the country you always dreamed about? Now you can stop dreaming.

'There was a flight ticket attached—God, you won't believe how excited I was, when he picked me up at the airport. I felt like a bloody teenager, and that was before he told me about the lottery, and the vineyard he'd bought for us to run together. I physically pinched my arm when we drove through those wrought iron gates and up the long, gravel drive to this. Honestly, Gabriel, I thought I'd died and gone to heaven.' The light in Melodie's eyes suddenly hardened. 'And what happens? The first face I see when we go inside is Faye's. I'll bet he even drove her over, too. That bitch never does one damn thing herself.' Melodie picked up the jade goddess that acted as a paperweight and hurled it at the wall. 'I'll give him Aphro-bloody-dite!'

Gabriel watched the warm September sun bathe vines that stretched out to infinity. If the police thought the women's feelings for the deceased revolved round hate, it was nothing compared to the anger and resentment they felt for one other—which is why it made no sense that any of them would kill Benjamin. Each other, *oui*. He wouldn't have thought twice, had it been one of their bodies lying dead in the cellar, or pushed down the stairs, or battered with a lump of firewood, or even throttled with finely manicured hands. But anger and resentment isn't enough to warrant wrapping clingfilm over someone's face. Holding it in place takes time, planning and commitment, not to mention the sheer physical effort. To lash out in the heat of the moment is one thing, but this? This was cold. Ice cold. Also, Gabriel would have noticed if any of the them had slipped away for that amount of time.

Wouldn't he?

'Sorry.' Melodie sheepishly picked up the paperweight, inspecting both it and the wall for chips. Considering jade, stone and goddesses had withstood thousands of years of weathering and abuse, it was hardly surprising that there wasn't so much as a blemish. 'The funny thing is, Beni said he chose this vineyard coz the statue reminded him of me.' She giggled. 'I said, I hope you don't mean shallow, love, coz that thing's polystyrene.'

Benjamin was livid, when he took possession of the vineyard. *Bastards stripped the place completely, Gabe! Everything from the sockets on the walls to the light fittings, the cooker, the plant pots, and what really got my goat was that they took the sculpture that defines the bloody wine.*

Ah, but he had to understand that this was France. If it wasn't listed on the contract of sale, then everything belonged to the seller, it was their right to take it. Morality was a different matter.

'Apparently the family wanted ze original for its sentimental value.'

Melodie snorted. 'You mean its retail value, being marble.'

Gabriel was inclined to agree, but what's done is done, there was no going back. His eyes followed a hare scampering between two rows of vines. People said Benjamin bought the vineyard for all the wrong reasons, and in many respects they were right. The subtleties of *terroir*, aspect and climate washed right over him. Vintages didn't concern him. Grape varieties? who cared? And as for the different *appellations…!*

Non, he pitched his tent here, having fallen in love with the endless rolling hills, the mild, sunny climate, and that, in his eyes, St Emilion wasn't synonymous with wine. *Au contraire.* He was captivated by this beautiful medieval gem, whose steep, narrow streets were lined with timber framed houses, and which boasted an underground church carved into the rock. For the same reason, Bordeaux conjured up a sweeping, elegant city, full of bridges, spires and fountains, while he was attracted to *Aphrodite* for the honey-coloured stonework dripping with purple wisteria, offset against dazzling white shutters. He liked the hand-drawn label on the bottle, depicting the goddess atop her dais, with a ring of neatly clipped box trees at her feet. He found peace—who wouldn't?—in the silence and solitude of the cool, dark, earthy cellars where the wine was aged in gigantic oak barrels. And he was tickled pink (whatever that meant) by the circular stone tower that once housed pigeons, whose droppings fertilised the soil. Most of all, though, he was drawn to the idea of being in charge of his own destiny, and often joked that if he never saw another motorway services in his life, it would be too soon.

So *oui*. Benjamin's motives not might be conventional, but *mon dieu*, that man had passion. Determined to turn *Aphrodite's* fortunes around, he advertised for an expert to manage the estate and who, over the course of time, could teach him the process of wine making inside out. Not for him, playing lord of the manor. He wanted to be hands-on from literally the ground up, even if that involved back-breaking pruning, de-budding, and tying back the vines, often in sub-zero temperatures dawn to dusk. Unfortunately, that same passion drove him to overspend, and by the time Gabriel took up the reins, almost every penny of the lottery win had gone. Much of it had been swallowed up by paying over the odds for the vineyard, the rest by throwing money at all the wrong things.

That's why you're here, Gabe, to keep the finances on track, but what's Château d'Aphrodite without its goddess? Château Empty Pole, that's what.

Gabriel sympathised with what Benjamin felt was a swindle, but right now, the priority was getting the business back on its feet before splashing out to replace expensive marble statues. Plastic (not polystyrene!) was less than ideal, but once it was impaled on that sad, empty pole, the only people who would ever know the difference were the workers on the estate. Who'd just be grateful for a job.

Long after Melodie left, he remained at the window, gazing across vines that stretched to infinity. Did any view define peace and calm better? Except appearances can be deceptive. Like swans on a river, paddling against a raging current yet all the time looking serene, the vines were also hard at work. Hectare upon hectare were quietly but industriously swelling their grapes to produce the right amount of sugar to yield the right amount of alcohol in the late summer heat, while simultaneously juggling acids, tannins and other chemical compounds to create the perfect balance for the wine. Another month, though, and this peace and calm would be a distant memory. The deer, boar and hares that called these vines home would seek refuge in the woods—but the harvest was just the start of the frenzy. After picking, the grapes needed to be sorted, to ensure no unripe or rotten fruit went into the crusher, though these days, mechanical presses did all the hard work. They looked traditional—the spitting image of old wooden wine presses—but behind the facade, they were very much state-of-the-art. But oh, how Benjamin excited was, about mastering the art of fermentation. How keen he'd been to learn how clarification of the wine came about. Before bottling his very first vintage…

An ache filled Gabriel's heart. Would he still be here to supervise the delicate filtering process his friend had so very much been looking forward to? To oversee the young wine being transferred into oak barrels to age?

He tidied away the last of the paperwork, locked the safe, and did a quick reconciliation of the company's bank balance, all on automatic pilot. Because the only thing he could think about was what he wouldn't give to see the next generation of *Château d'Aphrodite* being bottled, then raising a toast to his friend—secure in the knowledge that justice had been served and a killer brought to book.

Which, right now, seemed impossible.

* * *

'I'm not going to his funeral.' Chloe pursed her lips to prove it. 'When they bury him tomorrow, I'll be wearing white from top to toe, I'll be drinking celebratory champagne, and praying that the miserable bastard rots in hell.'

Gabriel didn't hear her come down the steps of the cellar. Was that because, like Melodie, she was naturally light of foot? Or had Benjamin's daughter deliberately crept down the stairs to surprise him? The same way, perhaps, that she'd surprised her father?

You see, that was the puzzle. The *casse-tête* that kept him awake at night, and gnawed away during the day. How did the killer get their victim to sit down, then calmly tie his hands behind his back? He hadn't put up a struggle before the clingfilm was wrapped over his face, the post-mortem proved that, nor had he been knocked unconscious then heaved into the chair. Which, given his size compared to any of the women, would have been nothing short of a miracle anyway. *Non*, Benjamin took the seat willingly. But why?

If Gabriel could work that out, he might be able to figure out who killed his friend. Yet the idea that it might be either his wife, his girlfriend or his daughter defied belief. Was there something he didn't know…?

He had come down to the cellar, not to search for clues—there weren't any. The police found no trace evidence, and the only fingerprints down here were his, the women's, and of course Benjamin's. There were smudges, suggestive of someone wearing gloves, but entry—not to mention exit—was impossible. The instant Gabriel took control of the estate, he changed the locks, with just two keys cut for Benjamin and himself. Visitors and workers alike had to ring the bell for admittance, though once Benjamin confirmed that all three of his nearest and dearest were coming, Gabriel had three more keys cut. Except (and this was the conundrum) all of those were accounted for after the murder, while Gabriel's remained tucked firmly in his pocket, and Benjamin's was still on the keyring in his safe. So, with no clues to follow and hope fading fast, Gabriel had returned to the place where his friend gasped his last breath in the hope of finding some sense of reason.

'You're angry,' he told Chloe, 'and you 'ave every right. Your father brought you 'ere to explain, but 'e didn't get ze chance.'

'Explain what? How he expected to make up for twenty-four lost years by showering me with money, now that he was rolling in it?'

That was the first thing the police thought, when this rich Englishman was murdered. The motive had to be financial. That was until Gabriel showed them the accounts, proving that the funds were tied up in property and the bank balance was, in fact, precariously low.

'Or did he bring me here to explain why he dumped my mum the second he found out she was pregnant, then threatened her with lawsuits and god-knows-what, if she ever breathed a word that he was my father?'

Chloe grabbed a bottle from the rack that ran floor to ceiling, wall to wall, round the cellar, and weighted it in her hand.

'Please don't. I've only just finished clearing up a century of dust and box leaves and spiders' webs. I'd rather not have to mop up wine as well.'

Chloe almost laughed. 'I wasn't going to throw it, Monsieur Larroque—'

'Gabriel.'

'I came down to find something to drink. Got a corkscrew?'

'That's a 2005, and it needs to breathe. If you want a wine to drink now, you want zis.' He selected a bottle from the opposite wall, along with a glass from the cabinet.

'If it's all the same with you, I'd rather not drink alone.'

'You know—' He tilted the glass to one side, holding it up to the neutral light, geared to test for colour and viscosity '—ze bark of your companions upstairs is a lot worse than their bite.'

'If you think I'm having anything to do with the scheming bitch who put him up to threatening my mother, then put her mark on him with marriage, much less Scheming Bitch 2.0 who stole him from Faye, you're bonkers.'

See? English people *do* make up words to annoy foreigners.

Gabriel carefully inhaled the fragrant complex of aromas, from the oak in which the wine aged, through to the earthy notes of truffle, musk and leather. ''E didn't.'

'Didn't what?'

'Abandon your mother when she was pregnant.' Gabriel dragged his focus away from the blend. 'Benjamin only met Faye ten years ago, zey married one year later. Melodie was a shoulder to cry on after Faye came out as gay, and the first time 'e found out about you was last November.'

'I don't believe you.'

'You don't 'ave to.' He drew a letter from his back pocket, still in its envelope addressed to "Benjamin Hardcastle, Lottery Winner, Hampshire".

Just like Santa Claus, Gabe. He could almost hear his friend's throaty chuckle in this carefully controlled temperature setting. *All the correspondence gets delivered eventually. I got sackfuls of the stuff every day.*

'Ohmygod.' Blood drained from Chloe's face as she slumped against the wall. Because the contents of the letter was a shock? Because she killed the man she thought had abandoned her and her mother? Or a combination of both…? 'Have—have you read it?'

'Your father showed it to me, after ze results of the DNA came through.'

Benjamin wouldn't have wanted his daughter to see the letter, *pas du tout*, but he was dead, she was alive, and Gabriel felt that she deserved the truth.

Which was that her mother had lied to her for twenty-four years.

She was the one who ended the relationship, not Benjamin, when she found out she was pregnant, then invented a story—a series of stories, in fact—to paint him in the worst possible light. Quite why was a mystery. Benjamin said she had a controlling personality. Perhaps it was simply a case of not wanting to share her child? At least, not until she read in the papers about him winning the lottery, then wrote to him, asking for money.

Twenty-four years of missed child support, Gabe. That's what she wants, because that's all I am to her. A pay-out. But what about me? My whole life all I've ever wanted was to be a dad—ask Faye. That's what triggered her coming out. Now I find I've been cheated out of twenty-four years.

He requested DNA tests. Obviously. And while he could never forgive the deceit, when all was said and done, he did have a daughter…

A beautiful, bright, vibrant kid, Gabe. I'm so bloody proud of her, the way she carved her own path in life.

Defying her mother's wishes to pursue a prestigious career in the city (by which she presumably meant the best-paying), Chloe followed her dream of work in the hospitality industry. Dreams that crashed when COVID-19 killed the hotel trade.

How much time passed before she stopped crying, gulping, cursing her mother? Who knows? Down in this cool, dark, underground world time stood still, because the only marker of change was when a new vintage was added. Right now, though, there was no room even for that. The ensuing financial crisis had banked up stocks to an alarming degree, and if something wasn't done, and soon, *Aphrodite* would collapse into memory.

'He really did want to make up for lost time, didn't he? It wasn't about the money at all.' Chloe had already slugged back half a bottle. It didn't stop her reaching for a refill. 'I should have guessed when I read the date of the harvest.'

'September 25th?'

'That's my birthday, Gabriel. Don't you see? He set the harvest especially for me.'

Actually, to qualify for the *appellation*, the date differed year by year, depending on the spring and summer weather. But regardless of how much it rained (or didn't), how hot it was (or wasn't), one hundred days after the vines flowered—exactly one hundred days—the grapes were scientifically assessed for size and appearance, then a precise date fixed for the harvest.

There was nothing to gain by pointing that out.

'Benjamin was a good man, Chloe. 'E made mistakes. We all do.' A fierce twinge shot through him, as he remembered his own short, failed marriage. 'But 'e was determined to make zings right with all three of you.'

Only he wasn't given the chance, and for that, Gabriel would curse his killer to the grave and beyond. No one has the right to take a life, especially in such a horrific way. He couldn't imagine the terror of those final moments, which made it even harder to fathom out who killed him, how or why—

Mon Dieu. He dropped to his knees, and began sifting through the sweepings he'd been clearing up before Chloe tiptoed down the stairs. Spiders' webs, box leaves, dust. Was it possible…? The theory was wild. Outrageous, even. But it was the only thing that made sense—

'What are you doing?'

'Looking for justice.'

He would need to check a couple of details, but if he was right, Gabriel knew exactly who killed his friend, along with the how and the why.

* * *

Benjamin Hardcastle didn't know much about women. If he had, he wouldn't have tried to make things right with his wife, his girlfriend and his estranged daughter in the south of France. Leastways, not all at the same time.

The trouble was, Benjamin Hardcastle was a romantic through to his marrow. He'd held this optimistic belief that the three women he loved most in his life (apart from his mother, God rest her soul) would bond over this magnificent vineyard, its fabulous location, and his request for forgiveness all round. Faye would see Melodie for the competent, sharp businesswoman that she really was. Melodie would have no reason to be jealous of his ex, since he intended to propose. Chloe couldn't fail to be won over by them both.

As acts of contrition go, it was naive in the extreme, but *hein.* Knowing Benjamin, it might—just might—have worked.

Sure, the faux fur's gonna fly, Gabe. He'd pulled a comic face. *And I doubt Manolo hitting shin bone is a sound these oak barrels are familiar with, but trust me, they'll come around. I know it.*

His reasoning was simple. Once the girls fell in love with the place the way that he had, and understood that it was their home as much as his now, friendships would develop. That was why he'd hung on to the divorce papers, even though he'd signed them ages back. He wanted to hand them to Faye in person, not through some soulless legal process, and tell her face to face that he would always love her, albeit in a different way, and that he was proud of her. It took guts, coming out as gay after struggling with her sexuality for so long, and he was wrong about Bianca, too. He'd seen street artists in Bordeaux, and the patience, strength and dedication it took to balance on a tiny seat attached to a pole for hours on end to appear suspended in mid-air was beyond admirable. They didn't pose head to foot in gold or bronze without moving for the money! Theirs was a vocation, not a job, and the pleasure they gave passers-by was immeasurable.

There's no price on making people happy, Gabe.

And making Melodie happy was right up there on his list. After the break-up of his marriage, he hadn't expected to fall in love, and certainly not so soon. But very quickly he realised there had been something lacking in his relationship with Faye, and the missing piece was trust. That she hadn't been able to confide her pain was down to him, or so he believed, which was why he spent so much time renovating the marital home. If his marriage hadn't run perfectly, then a house that did would make up for it. Right—?

I didn't tell Melodie about the lottery, because I didn't want her to think I could buy my way back. I needed to find a way to knock her for six, and the second I saw the label, Gabe, that was it. My own Aphrodite in a bottle!

While Chloe, he reasoned, was simply a matter of time. Of getting to know one another, one step at a time, and slowly establishing trust.

Jeez, she even looks like me. Same mannerisms, too.

Benjamin Hardcastle was a romantic to his core, and that was the trouble. His heart ruled his head, but he should have trusted his instincts.

If he had, Benjamin Hardcastle would still be alive.

* * *

'You're working late.'

'Not working,' Gabriel told the new owner. 'Zinking.'

Night had wrapped her soft cloak over the vineyard, sending bats swooping for moths, while hedgehogs scuttled around in the undergrowth. Stretching his neck upwards on the terrace, he watched the Milky Way swirl across the blackness. Out in the woods, a fox barked, and a barn owl ghosted past on silent, white wings.

'About the harvest?'

'Not really.'

The yield was proving exceptionally good, thanks to late rain followed by a brief burst of heat, though this was not the harvest that kicked off on Chloe's birthday. Two years had passed since then, during which time, and under Gabriel's guidance, the new owners had made sweeping changes. For one thing, instead of employing an army of migrant workers to pick the grapes by hand, they'd hired a massive mechanical beast to do the job. Previously, this had been deemed too rough on the grapes, stripping them from the bunches as they hung on the vine, to leave what were effectively little green skeletons dangling. But this was before COVID. Before traditional outlets dried up. Before competition between the survivors turned brutal.

To turn the business around, innovative ideas were called for, new markets needed to be found, and production had to complement the direction the vineyard was taking. This didn't mean shortcuts. For instance, yeasts were vital to the fermentation process, but Gabriel wasn't the first wine-maker to kill off the natural, but erratic, yeasts in favour of custom-built strains to ensure more predictable results. Even so. For *Aphrodite* to re-establish herself in the trade, she needed more than just a few tweaks to old practices, and since she couldn't take the wine to as many customers as she'd like, there was only one other option. Bring the customers to the wine.

'I was zinking how proud my friend would 'ave been of 'is vineyard.'

There was zero chance of reversing his financial impulses, but a massive cash injection from the new owners was enough to convert the *Château* into a warm and welcoming hotel. A magnet for those in search of fine wines, stunning architecture, amazing art and untouched villages, where guests could relax, unwind, and enjoy wine tasting, both on site and on tours, amid fine weather and shimmering 360° views. To achieve this, an army of tradesmen had laboured round the clock, knocking walls down here, putting walls up there, installing lighting, plumbing, fittings, you name it, transforming the house and outbuildings at dizzying speed. With a work ethic after Benjamin's own heart, the new owners also pitched in, no job too menial, no hours too long, with the result that *Aphrodite* was already looking at ninety percent occupancy in high season.

Not such an obscure vineyard, after all.

There was talk, too, of adding a swimming pool and converting the circular stone *pigeonnier* into self-contained apartments, same as the stables, as well as ways to attract corporate events in the off season. But one thing was unanimous. Plastic statues were out of the question. Once again, a marble goddess stood tall on her dais, a ring of neatly clipped box trees at her feet.

'I think your friend would be more proud that you put a cold-blooded killer behind bars.'

Cold. *Oui.* That was what troubled Gabriel from the start.

'Hot emotions, like anger and resentment, often erupt into murder,' he said. 'But not zis time.'

They were—how could he have missed it?—the classic signs of grief. He watched a shooting star zing over the horizon. The best time to catch meteor showers was mid-August, but a clear night like this? You could count the panels on the weather satellites twenty thousand miles up.

'It was only when I swept up the mountain of dust zat I understood.'

Once he had the why, the who became obvious, and the how quickly fell into place.

'There was no reason for box leaves to be in the cellar, and zat's when I realised ze killer was driven by greed, pure and simple.'

When Faye came out as gay, there was no jumping and shouting and singing from the rafters. *Au contraire.* She slithered out, ashamed of holding her secret for so long, embarrassed at how friends and family might react, guilty for stringing her husband along. It was only when he talked about starting a family that she had to come clean, for her own sake as well as his, but it left her vulnerable and raw in the process. Easy prey for a predator.

All Bianca does is take, take, take, Gabe.

Melodie resented Faye for treating him like her personal handyman, but what she hadn't seen—how could she?—was how Bianca had manipulated Faye, slowly and systematically exerting control over every aspect of her life.

I'll bet he even drove her here, Melodie had snapped. *That bitch never does one damn thing herself.*

Only because Bianca had suffocated her spirit, and made her completely reliant. When Gabriel suggested the police check whether Faye had actually used the flight ticket Benjamin sent, he wasn't surprised to hear that she and Bianca had driven over together. Or that Bianca had booked herself into a nearby hotel…

The only reason she stands still all day is coz she's too bleedin' lazy to get a proper job.

Why should she? To all outwards appearances, Faye was the same dynamic sales manager for a large food processing corporation that she always had been. She banked a good salary, half-owned a lovely home in a pleasant residential area, with an ex-husband who could, thanks to Bianca pulling the strings, also be manipulated into thinking the marital house was his responsibility. Leaving Bianca free to indulge her passion for *tableaux vivants*—another outlet for control, except in this case over her own body, pushing herself to her physical limits.

'A few basic checks was all zat was needed.'

With no other family, who was listed as Benjamin's next of kin? Faye. And who had a key cut at the local DIY store? Bianca.

The smoky smell of wild mushrooms drifted on the warm night air, along with the chirrup of tree frogs, and the rasp of cicadas that would be deafening, had the woods been any closer.

'So—' The new owner sighed. 'On the night of the get-together, she hid in the boot of the car.'

'Once through ze gates, away from the cctv, she slid the statue off on its pole and took its place—same way she did every day in ze park or ze High Street.'

'Later, when she knew the five of us would be in *le salon*, Bianca replaced the statue, let herself in with the key, then crept down to ze cellar to wait.'

How did he know? For one thing, the unusual amount of white dust, which, when forensics tested it, turned out to be, *oui*, body paint residue.

But ze box leaves were the clincher.

'Benjamin clipped zem right before the big day, so *le Château* would look picture perfect.'

Inevitably, being fresh, some of the clippings would be left behind. Equally inevitably, some would stick to Aphrodite's hem.

'Time, zen, for Bianca to draw on 'er performance skills.'

Because that was another thing Gabriel hadn't been able to fathom. Why Benjamin allowed himself to be trussed up like a chicken.

'If it was a robber, even armed with a knife, 'e would have rushed him.'

Not to protect his wines, or even his pride. But because Benjamin Hardcastle would lay down his life before he risked the welfare of the three people he loved most in the world.

'On ze other hand, if it was someone 'e knew…? Someone who told 'im she wanted to mend bridges…?'

Someone who suggested playing the perfect practical joke? *Aphrodite* holding him to ransom for treating her divine image disgracefully?

'Desperate to make amends, 'e went along with the prank.'

Actually thought it was brilliant, they found out afterwards. In fact, was still laughing when Bianca wound the clingfilm over his face.

'Ah, there you are!'

The other two owners emerged from the house, one carrying a plate of *apèros*—wafer thin Bayonne ham, *saucisson*, olives, *foie gras*—the other balancing a bottle of wine and four glasses. Gabriel did the honours, and poured.

Bianca's plan was cunning, ingenious, daring and, credit where it was due, pretty near fool-proof. Since Faye had a water-tight alibi, nothing stood between her inheriting the jackpot, once the will had been settled.

'To Benjamin,' he said, raising his glass. 'A good man and a good friend, who deserved life more zan justice.'

'Here, here!'

But even as the glasses chinked under the stars, his blood chilled. Bianca was this close to getting away with murder. What were the odds, then, of Faye meeting with a fatal accident in a year or so's time?

'To a great husband!'

'A terrific partner!'

'My father!'

Because that's where Bianca's plans fell flat. What she didn't know— none of them did—was that Benjamin bequeathed his vineyard in equal parts to all three women.

'I don't think I'll ever find love again,' Faye said quietly.

'You won't 'ave to.' Gabriel smiled. 'Love will find you.'

'The way it did you?'

He said nothing, but the softness in his eyes, as he glanced over her shoulder to where Chloe was clearing space for the *apèros*, spoke volumes. After the pain of divorce, he hadn't expected to fall for anyone ever again, but twirling tender tendrils round wire, shoulder to shoulder, checking for frost damage, mildew, mites, rust and mealybugs, brings people together.

Even more surprising, though, was the three of them actually working together. He was sure they'd sell up and go their separate ways, and, to be fair, so did they. Except none of them felt good about abandoning ship right before Benjamin's precious harvest, and the same sense of loyalty that saw them gathering grapes guided them through the rest of the wine-making process.

Melodie was the first to admit she was wrong. Faytal Attraction hadn't set out to engineer her split from Benjamin at all, and soon she came to see the bitchiness for what it really was. Envy of the contentment that her ex-husband had found.

For her part, Faye fully expected the others to hate her, Melodie most of all. She'd deliberately portrayed her as shallow and empty-headed, when the woman ran her own salon, for God's sake! Taking on every aspect of the maintenance herself, and preserving her success through lockdown and recession, while still remaining cheerful and upbeat. In fact, it was that same practicality and resourcefulness that allowed Melodie to pick up the commercial aspects of the vineyard with such speed.

Sowing the seeds for a new path for *Aphrodite* to follow.

Once the girls fall in love with the place the way I did, and understand that it's their home as much as mine, friendships will develop, Gabe—trust me.

Mon Dieu, they developed deeper than Benjamin could have imagined. Take Melodie's management skills, add Faye's talent in sales then throw in Chloe's experience in the hospitality industry, and there was no stopping them.

'I still can't understand the gobbledygook on the bottle,' Chloe said, squinting at the label in French.

'Me neither,' Melodie trilled, 'but the stuff inside's scrumptious!'

'I'll drink to that,' Faye said. 'Chin-chin and mud-in-yer-eye!"

Gabriel turned back to the Milky Way, coursing slowly through the heavens, and once more raised his glass to his friend. Benjamin Hardcastle might not have known much about women, but he knew enough to invite the right ones to share his world, both in life and in death.

He still wished English people would stop making up words to annoy foreigners, though.

Drawn to Murder

'Rune stones?' Ellen could only imagine what people would say, if she told them. 'You're not seriously saying the rune stones made you do it?'

Realistically, was it so surprising? From her parents to her brother, to her friends, her clients, her neighbours and her lying, cheating ex, no one would expect this level-headed, self-employed book-keeper to blame a bunch of rocks carved with mysterious ancient symbols. But what other explanation was there?

Until she rolled up in this tiny town on the Swedish archipelago, Ellen had never owned a sketch book in her life. She'd hated art at school, never so much as doodled in the margins as a kid, and, being a thoroughly practical girl, never saw the point of paper anyway. Now look. A wander into one of Sigtuna's painted wooden shops, more out of curiosity than any urge to buy, and out she comes, armed with everything a sketch artist could possibly need. And the urge to fill blank pages with a passion!

Pushing her thick, blonde mane away from her face, she took a seat beside one of the hundred and seventy standing stones in question. Sigtuna wasn't just Sweden's oldest town, but its original Viking capital, making it a walking, talking history museum, with a spectacular location on the lake. And the amazing part about all this? She actually had a talent for capturing the runic lettering, the honey coloured ruins of the monasteries and churches, the model-village-sized town hall that was, unsurprisingly, the smallest civic hall in Europe.

Three weeks down the line, and no eccentricity had escaped Ellen's pencil. Not the cut-out metal moose which, from the right angle, appeared to be a live animal wading through the water. Not the wooden bell tower on the hill, that, no matter *which* angle you looked at that from, was still a Dalek in a skirt. And certainly not the famous dragon tree, OK just a fallen branch with the thin end carved to resemble the head of a dragon—but one that fired the imagination of every child who flew, or tamed, or rode it.

'Sketching?' Ryan would have sneered. 'Waste of bloody time, if you ask me. Where's the colour? Where's the sharpness?' That was him all over, though. Everything was about instant results, and just because he salivated over shutter speeds and apertures didn't mean she had to. Then again, when had he ever cared what Ellen really wanted? It was typical that he'd bought her the most expensive camera on the market as his way of saying sorry that he'd cheated on her.

'It was just a fling. It didn't mean anything, Ells, I swear to God.'

'Five months is a long time to drag out something meaningless,' she'd murmured, packing up her things. 'Especially with one of my clients.'

'No, no, look! This shows how much I love you, babes,' he said, clipping on the lenses, lining up imaginary shots. 'Me, you, this camera, we can take a holiday. Australia. New Zealand. Singapore. Think of the memories we'll make with this!'

Well done, Ryan. Knew the price of everything and the value of nothing. Driving to her mother's, she'd taken great pleasure in dropping that expensive piece of apology in the Thames, but heyho, that was more than two years ago. Twenty-seven months, to be precise, in which time the hurt had faded, the anger long gone, and even the most crushing sense of failure can't compete with the exactitude of balance sheets and the complexities of the Inland Revenue. All the same, no one was more surprised than Ellen to find she'd come through the divorce happier and stronger, but (and here's the irony) in need of a new focus.

Opening her pad, she began to sketch the waterlilies that embroidered the water's edge. Pencilled in the mother duck paddling past with seven—no, good grief, *ten* fluffy little ducklings. Smiled as the last one put a spurt on to catch up. At some stage, she'd have to get back in the dating saddle. Right now, though, the prospect filled her with dread. OK, at thirty-four, she still had a good figure. But only because time spent at the gym meant less time in her poky, rented flat, while eating alone was more for nutrition than for pleasure. In any case, dating's about more than looks, and for proof, look no further than her sketch book.

At the start, she came to this spot, same time every day, simply to soak up the long, warm rays of a sun that, like a naughty child, never wanted to go to bed up here just below the Arctic circle. But rather than sketch the low stone circle or the inlet beyond, where swallows dipped low and the white sails of yachts floated past, her brave little pencil found it could also capture the essence of character, a prime example being the lanky, handsome man and his succession of hapless dates. And now one thing was certain. Having seen the…let's be kind and say "eclectic" results of what was obviously on-line dating, that's one road that would never be for her. Not in a million bloody years!

She flipped back through the pages. Nope, not the eighteenth century copper tents designed to resemble a Sultan's encampment at the edge of the forest. Not the Viking longboat, either, or the old early crofters' cottages. Aha, here we go. Number 1 in a series of what she called *Date Fright*, starring Sven (the first Swedish name she could think of), and that's why she kept coming back here every evening. Not because he was film star hot, but because he, too, had a habit of turning up at the same time three or four times a week, carrying a gift-wrapped box tied up with ribbon. Chocolates, would be her guess, unimaginative, but safe, to meet what he obviously hoped would be That Special Someone.

With every encounter, there'd be the same nod and handshake, all terribly Scandinavian and formal, which her pencil captured in all its awkwardness. Given his rugged looks, you'd think it would be Sven, not the women, who'd be pissed off at finding their date had posted a picture taken fifteen years ago, blithely imagining everyone did the same. On the contrary. You only had to look at that very first sketch to see the embarrassment on the poor cow's face. Biting her lip. Close to tears with the shame. Number 2 was the youngest, but Ellen's pencil captured how she'd kept glancing over her shoulder, obviously worried that someone was watching. (Don't you just love an adulterous assignation!) While Number 3 was so mortified by the age gap that she hunched into her clothes, hopng for all the world to disappear.

And so it went on. Women of all shapes and race and age, meeting their hot date beside the sacred circle, where they'd sit for a few minutes, talking so earnestly that at one point Ellen wondered if he wasn't perhaps a journalist, the way he seemed to interrogate them. But then he'd squeeze their shoulder, hand them the chocolates, and the happy couple would stroll off, arms linked, down the little lane beside the lake that didn't actually go anywhere, but was merely access for the handful of houses whose back gardens faced the water.

Half an hour later, sometimes less, by which time the light had faded, swallows had given way to bats, and the lake had turned to ink, Sven would saunter back alone, and who could blame him? On-line dating was a lottery, which few people ever won. Ellen flicked through the pages. Either the poor sod had been suckered into believing the only way to find a soulmate was through the internet, or he had a serious gambling addiction. Either way, she shuddered at the prospect of having to create a profile, then sitting by her laptop until—

Wait!

Wait, wait, wait, wait, wait…

She jolted upright. What's the one thing his dates had in common? She checked her sketches to make sure, but yes, every single one lacked confidence. And not the usual nervousness that someone new to the dating game might have. This was genuine insecurity. Witness the tense introductions. The earnest responses to what, she imagined, were pretty innocuous questions. The timid way they (without exception) took his arm a few minutes later.

But, and this was what made Ellen sit up—what else did these women have in common?

Exactly. They all went on the Road to Nowhere with him.

None of them came back.

* * *

Stop, Ellen told herself. *You've been watching way too much TV!* She'd walked that short stretch of road a dozen times, it was delightful. With virtually no traffic, since the only cars were the owners of those pretty painted wooden houses, or else access to a boat ramp on a tiny inlet, with parking for half a dozen cars at most. After that it became a foot and cycle path that led all the way to Stockholm's international airport, so why wouldn't strangers crave a little privacy on their first date? God knows, the owners of the houses wanted it. Look at those tall evergreens that offered dense seclusion from the lane! And while their balconies had fabulous views across the water, none of the occupants could be seen by people passing underneath.

Even so. Ellen pored back over the drawings, at the gift-wrapped chocolates, his easy walk, the stiff gait of the women. *Blind date nerves, that's all. Don't overthink this!* Then she remembered Ted Bundy. Handsome, affable, eminently trustworthy…right up to the point when he wasn't.

Another one who'd perfected the art of abducting his victims in plain sight.

Who would suspect this tall, rugged stranger? Not the picnickers, tucking into sandwiches of shrimp, pickled herrings and cured salmon. Not the laughing families tangling with the mini-golf, or parents, keeping a worried eye on their kids clambering over the dragon. And certainly not the hordes of tourists taking selfies with the rune stones! Sigtuna might not be the bustling trading hub it used to be, but its quaint narrow streets and old wooden houses made it a tourist hot spot, where strangers pass through all the time.

She checked her watch. If he was coming, Sven would be parking his car any second—*yep*. From the corner of her eye, she watched him reach across to the passenger seat, pick up the chocolates (pink wrapping with a silver bow tonight), before heading for the same bench facing the water. Her pencil captured him with both arms draped over the back of the seat, legs crossed. Was this really the demeanour of a man who lured vulnerable women to secluded spots before assaulting them, knowing they'd be too ashamed to report it?

Too many CSI's, Ellen. Stick to book-keeping! She rolled her eyes. If only. For twenty-seven tense unyielding months, she'd waited for the divorce to finalise so she could buy herself a decent place and finally move on, and what happens? The day it comes through, she closes her business, gives up her rented flat, and puts everything she owns into storage. Freewheeling for the first time in her life, syncing to a rhythm that was the opposite of anything she was used to—and perhaps that explained the obsession to sketch? A need to keep the pace slow, but concentration levels high? Was it still the old case of "you can run but you can't hide" that was driving her to turn her old life on its head? Or because there was no dirt, no noise, no pressure in her life here? Just solitude, space, a pad that was filling up fast—and a bunch of rune stones that tied this town to its mysterious past. And made her imagination run wild.

Even so. As her pencil copied the whorls, swirls and curls, then added the strange symbols that encased these red, interwoven spirals, Ellen was conscious of a skinny brunette climbing out of a taxi. This time, though, she didn't sketch the discomfort and the awkward introductions. She quietly stowed her gear in her back pack, before following them with nonchalance down the Road to Nowhere.

* * *

With no construction or development along most of the archipelago, it was easy to picture Viking longships cutting a sleek path through the water, their red and white striped sails billowing on the wind. To smell the wood from the smokehouses that dotted the shoreline, while fishermen mended their nets, hides dried in the sun, and huge vats bubbled with dye over the fires. Sigtuna was where Sweden's first coins were minted, filling the air with the clang of the smith's hammer, overriding even the strong monastic chants, since Christianity had been entrenched here from its founding. The 12th century thatches were long gone, but the higgledy-piggledy cream, white and falun-red houses that defined this town dated back centuries. All it needed was a cart, pulled by an ox and loaded with hay, and you'd be forgiven for thinking time had stood still.

Except Sigtuna wasn't a time capsule, and nothing was what it seemed.

In Viking times, the town bordered the Baltic. Today, thanks to a rising land mass, that particular arm of the sea was now a freshwater lake, whose tranquillity belied bloodthirsty raids from what are now Estonia, Latvia and Finland.

There was no magic in the rune. Despite the mystique, they were nothing more than tributes to chieftains, who—to ruin the illusion even further—were alive at the time, writing their own hype, and erecting the monuments themselves.

More pertinently, though, there was no trace of Sven or his date.

* * *

Two adults don't disappear into thin air. Ellen repeated the mantra as she retraced her steps. *They have to be here somewhere.*

So where? The narrow path that continued from the end of the lane was deserted. Just a lone cyclist in the distance, heading towards town. One of the houses? If so, why leave his shiny black Volvo in the car park? Backtracking, cursing herself for not following closer, she pretended to stretch her hamstring at every back gate. Each was locked. Same for the garages and boatsheds, while the boat ramp had been in full sight all the time, and in any case the only vessel that had ventured close was one of the ubiquitous white-sailed yachts that featured in every drawing, and had sailed right past the little inlet. One day, Ellen had tried to count the yachts, and failed, and that was one of the first things that struck her. Whether it was sailing, canoeing or paddleboards, the Swedes did like their water sports! Right down to the swimming and diving platforms that dotted the shoreline, and good luck with that, she thought. The water was a whole lot deeper than it looked, and when it came to plunging into glacial waters, she'd pass, thanks all the same.

Oh, come on, this isn't Wonderland, where he and Alice slid down a rabbit—well, well, well. Guess whose athletic stride just emerged from the rocks! Ellen broke into a run. No chocolates + no companion = victim still there. Terrified, cowering, bullied into believing it was his word against hers. Well, not any more, pal. Not with Ellen's pencilled evidence backing it up!

Fading light made it difficult to make out any kind of sharp detail, but as luck would have it, she'd explored this little tree-lined clearing three weeks ago, entranced by the water lilies and moorhens hugging the shore, its elegant lime trees, shimmering hazels and tall pine that had been hit by lightning at least three times (how unlucky can you get?) Little had she realised, on that earlier visit, that behind the clearing was a diving platform. Even tonight, when she heard the splash, it didn't click. But on reflection, where better than a secluded spot by the lake to assault a trusting date? Squinting in the twilight, stumbling more than once, Ellen scrambled over the boulders, ears pricked for the sound of sobbing, to—

What diving platform? Every inch of access to the water was flat, and despite the warm night air, she shivered.

Dear God, tell me that splash wasn't what I think it was.

* * *

Two days passed. Two days in which Ellen hadn't slept, hadn't eaten, had spent more time than was healthy going over that tiny peninsular with the finest of tooth combs. She had called and called and called in the fading light, but no one answered. She had searched and searched and searched for two days, but came up empty. The grass beside the water had been trampled, but there was no blood or gouges to indicate a struggle. No torn fabric. Zilch.

Dammit, she couldn't go to the police—and possibly ruin an innocent man's life—with just a dozen drawings and a splash. Suppose she was wrong?

She'd scoured the news for missing persons. Made polite, if slightly creepy, enquiries in the tourist office regarding crime rates. Was shocked to discover that Sweden wasn't anywhere near as safe as she thought, and that night time in Stockholm was actually safer than daylight when it came to be walking alone. Scouring the grasses and rocks for the umpteenth time (come on Lightning Tree, give me some help here!), she couldn't help wondering if the tail wasn't wagging the dog, because seriously. How many serial killers clock up three victims a week!

The ones who can get away with it, a little voice whispered...

The women arrived by taxi, ensuring there were no cars to trace back to missing persons. The airport was just ten miles away, was that important? Staring across the shimmering blue water, Ellen took a deep breath.

There was only one way to find out.

* * *

Right on cue, the Volvo pulled into the car park. Its lanky occupant emerged with his chocolates. Blue with gold ribbon. He locked up and strolled to his favourite bench. Heart pounding, Ellen sat beside him.

'Well, now.' Like everyone in Sweden, from waiting staff to bus drivers to supermarket cashiers, his English was perfect, with barely a hint of an accent. 'If it isn't my stalker.'

Oh. Shit.

'The sketch artist from Devon. Plymouth, am I right?' he continued, knowing damn well he was. 'Renting the yellow house with the white shutters and black ironwork on the corner by the gardens?'

'Now who's the stalker?' Fear disguised itself as indignation.

'Wouldn't you be curious to know who was watching *you*?'

No, no, no, this wasn't how it was supposed to go down. Ellen folded her hands so he couldn't see them shaking. 'I know what you do.'

'I don't doubt it for a second.' He tilted his head on one side and smiled. 'Accountants, by definition, must be accurate.'

Christ. How deep had he probed into her background? 'I'm a book-keeper, not an accountant.'

She'd lost the element of surprise. Been wrong-footed. Was more scared than she'd ever been in her life. But she was damned if she'd let it show, because predators like him thrive on fear. *Or do they?* Her gaze fixed on the lazy flight of a heron as she prayed the taxi delivering his date was held up in traffic, or, better still, that she'd missed the plane, if that's how she arrived, because Ellen was wrong. It wasn't fear that was these women's downfall. It was trust. A combination of looks, charm, even his calmness, had them eating out of his hand within a matter of minutes.

They'd call it sex appeal.

He'd call it total control.

'I know what you do, but so help me, that's the last time you've taken anyone on a one-way trip.' This time the anger was real. 'I'm calling the police.'

She reached for her phone, but a hand clamped round her wrist. 'That would be a mistake.'

'Then I'll scream so loud, other people will call the police.'

'I wouldn't do that, either.'

'Fine.' She'd snatched the box before he knew what was happening, and chocolates be damned. This was a serial killer's tool kit, gift-wrapped to deflect attention, and put his victims at ease. *What the hell did he promise these women?*

'Give it back, please.' His voice had the same hard edge as his eyes.

'Or what?'

'It doesn't belong to you, Ellen.' He nodded towards the taxi turning into the car park. 'It's for her.'

Ellen. He knew her name...

'That girl is not going with you.'

'It's what she wants.'

Finally, the squirming discomfort made sense. The women weren't ashamed or embarrassed at meeting a date as hot as his photo. Each was in anguish beyond breaking point, but where any half-decent human being would encourage them to seek help, this bastard incited them to take their own lives. Watching while the last breath left their bodies...and enjoying every last second.

He'd plead euthanasia, helping desperate souls escape hell. Nice try, pal. This was cold-blooded murder—and Ellen had the proof in her hands.

In the car park behind them, a blonde in dark glasses was stepping out of the taxi. Even from this distance, the port-wine birthmark on the side of her face stood out. Ellen's stomach flipped. Was the bullying so bad, that he'd gaslighted her into believing the only way to end it was to take her own life?

'For Christ's sake,' he hissed, 'she'll be here any second, now give me the box!'

'The hell I will.'

He lunged, she gripped, he grabbed, he won. The box shot through Ellen's fingers, the gold ribbon bursting apart in the struggle. As the lid flew off, papers scattered over the grass. Including a passport of a woman with a port-wine birthmark on her cheek...

Shit.

Shit, shit, bugger and shit.

'Oh my God, you provide these women with a new identity!'

'Of course. What did you think?' He laughed. 'That I'm some kind of Ted Bundy?'

'No! No, of course not!'

He was too busy stuffing the blonde's new life back into the box to notice Ellen's cheeks burning. 'If you'd checked me out as thoroughly as I checked out my stalker, you'd know that I'm a printer.'

A small step from printer to forger, he explained, and he was seven when his father threw his mother downstairs.

'I couldn't help her,' he said thickly, 'but I can help others like her.' He replaced the lid on the box and stuffed the torn gold ribbon in his pocket. 'Now are you you going to stand here all night with your mouth open, Ellen Pace, or are you coming to help my client take that boat to a place where her husband will never break her ribs again?'

Boat. That splash the other night was the anchor...

She looked into the eyes of the lanky man with the rugged good looks whose image adorned most of her sketch pad, and saw that those eyes were green. Later, Ellen blamed the dragon tree, the standing stones, but most especially the rune stones for what came out of her mouth next.

'Don't suppose you need a book-keeper, do you?'

But what other explanation was there?

Leap of Faith

Bernard made a fortune from committing suicide. Some might even say a killing.

* * *

I'm still waiting for those sales figures, Bernard.

Call this a report? My three-year old writes longer paragraphs!

You promised to have that presentation on my desk a week ago.

What a life. Mondays commuting to the office, wall-to-wall meetings and no time for lunch. Tuesdays, Wednesdays, Thursdays on the road, up at 5 a.m.to miss the traffic, nights in soulless motorway hotels in Manchester, Edinburgh, Cardiff, Brighton, never the same place twice. Fridays getting a bollocking from his boss, because those all-important sales were down, which meant, of course, weekends spent with PowerPoint and emails instead of friends and family.

Not, to be fair, that he had friends or family.

Hayley, hi, just wondered if you fancied meeting up for a—oh. Right. No, no, no, that's fine. Absolutely. Not a problem.

Jen, it's Bernard. I thought maybe we could try that new Italian restaurant on Friday—Sure, sure. Fully understand. Saturday? How about next Tuesday? Of course. Some other time, then.

Stella, it's me. You haven't returned my calls, so I—well, there's no need to be vulgar!

'Is it true that girls used to call you ugly, until they found out how much you earned?' his boss would joke. 'Now they call you ugly and poor?'

Ha bloody ha. So he was no Brad Pitt? So all that office work, and hunched up behind a steering wheel, left him a little on the flabby side?

Holy Christ, at thirty-eight, who wasn't?

For his employers—or more importantly, their shareholders—the world would end if it was the competition's pumps, not theirs, turning cocoa beans into chocolate, apples into cider, and milk into butter. Quite frankly, Bernard couldn't give a toss. Ringing round potential customers trying to make appointments, schmoozing existing customers with overpriced meals, and building presentations bored him witless. The problem was, having climbed the career ladder as far as he could go (and let's face it, that wasn't very far) he couldn't see an alternative. In fact, the only thing he *could* see was a lonely, empty spiral of nothingness, in which his only companions were food processing pumps. Who wouldn't want out of that?

'...body of a young woman was recovered this morning from the foot of Beachy Head. It is believed to be that of schoolteacher...'

Driving up the M6 past Stoke-on-Trent, Bernard was more concerned with traffic filtering on than the radio, but then, as the story unfolded, the desperation, the sadness, the very needlessness of this girl's suicide sank in. His life was bad, but Jesus Christ, how grim was hers, how bleak was her future, that she saw the only way to end the torment was to throw herself headfirst off a cliff? He felt for her, he truly did. All through the meetings, the negotiations, the dinners, the handshakes, her pain haunted him. He couldn't sleep for the emptiness that drove her to take her life, and in such a horrendous way. Crossing the Bristol suspension bridge a week later, his eyes filled at the courage she, and others like her, must have to draw on, and for the next three weeks, he stopped feeling sorry for himself, knuckled down to work, and accepted that life was never perfect.

Right up to the point where... actually...y'know... it could be...

* * *

Southend is hardly Damascus, but that was where the scales dropped from Bernard's eyes, and he saw his future mapped out rich and clear. Emphasis on the rich.

For those of you who don't know, Southend boasts the longest pleasure pier in the world. Extending over two kilometres into the Thames Estuary—1.34 miles if you prefer—it's been attracting visitors since 1833. And the reason it's so long? Mud flats. Mud flats mean shallow water, which in turn mean no docking facilities. Without docking facilities, boats carried Londoners escaping the Industrial Revolution straight past to neighbouring resorts, but with a pier boasting a pavilion at the end, and a railway leading up, Southend boomed. Its nineteenth century charm's long gone, but when you're cooped up inside, it's a treat to breathe in clean, salty air and stretch the legs at the end of the day.

Leaning on the rail, munching fish and chips out of the wrapper and watching the water gurgle round the pillars, he was vaguely aware of a kid—ten, maybe eleven—lugging a giant boulder off the train. Then he heard the plop. Knew instinctively that it was the sound of heavy rock hitting water and chips spilled across the boards. Where's the boy? Where's the kid? No, no, no, no, no—

Racing to the side, his knees went weak when he saw the little sod with a companion at the south side of the pier, tossing a similar boulder into the sea. Not a death jump. Just a competition as to who could make the loudest splash.

Little buggers.

Torn between laughing and snarling (that was his bloody dinner on the planks) was Bernard's lightbulb moment. In that split second, he saw a way to make a fortune and be answerable to no one, except himself.

Little by little, day by day, he began researching the psychology of suicide, along with understanding the support available to those contemplating that awful path. Even so, the first time he committed suicide he was terrified. Standing on the bridge, clutching a bag of rocks to his chest, he was, literally, shaking with fear.

'Don't do it!

'Don't jump!'

Jump? Were they crazy? Going off the Golden Gate Bridge in San Francisco you're talking speeds of 75mph. Not bloody likely, mate.

In the distance, sirens wailed, but the sirens weren't for him. Later he learned that in cases like this, they were never turned on, lest it spooked the poor sod into jumping. He could well believe it. You try keeping your balance on a narrow rail, balancing a sack of stones! As it happened the emergency services had already arrived, and after a suitably dramatic standoff, in other words enough time for videos and photos to break the internet, Bernard allowed himself to be talked down. *Now* there were sirens. Then hospitals, doctors, psychiatrists, more doctors, more psychiatrists, until finally the claim went in—*wham!* The system had failed this poor man, his lawyer argued. The bridge wasn't suicide proof, and moreover, his client had specifically told his GP more than once that life wasn't worth living, yet his client was sent home with nothing but anti-depressants and some number to ring. By the time he was counting the noughts on the settlement, Bernard had already scouted his next three jump sites.

A smooth rolling programme quickly evolved. While one claim was going through in, say, Aberdeen, he'd established emotional crises in Bristol, Leeds and Leicester, in fact any big, anonymous city, where doctors were so hideously overworked that there was no room for in-depth background checks.

Operation Pay Day wouldn't work if he was in prison.

If there was a downside, and only if, it was sitting through those endless rounds of counselling. Still. When it came to pulling anguished faces, picking at his nails, mumbling about dark voices deep inside, and how it was just too hard to talk about, he could have won an Oscar. Besides, avoiding eye contact with therapists was more than outweighed by the sun-drenched beaches of the Caribbean, rolling dice in Vegas, or floating round the Greek islands on a gin palace with hot girls in bikinis at his side. Not so ugly now.

A few years down the line—think of it as an apprenticeship—Bernard upped his game. It drew every inch of courage (and then some), but quadrupled compensation made it a no-brainer. By physically making the jump, it proved that he was committed to his objective, and while he still waited for kind hearts to rush forward, begging him not to follow through, let's talk it out, there has to be a better way, he needed to be absolutely bloody sure the first responders were bloody well on hand to respond.

Did it hurt, that first plunge? Was it cold? Was there blood? Truly, he had no idea. He was only aware of taking the biggest gamble of his life. Ashes to ashes. Dust to dust. Or, in his case, rocks to rocks. Then, oh thank you Jesus, he was in the air, gasping, wheezing, freezing, his shivering frame bundled in a blanket, before the circus kicked off again, only this time with a yacht of his own at the end. For the next few years, cruising the Adriatic and jetting off to Bali, Bernard counted every blessing, thanked every lucky star, and accepted that life could never be more perfect.

Right up to the point where... actually...y'know... it could...

* * *

'I'm so, so sorry! Are you all right?'

Not so much a case of bumping into her. More tripping over her as he stepped off his shiny Sunseeker motor yacht, hands in pockets and whistling, while deciding which of these fine restaurants in Antibes deserved his business.

'My fault entirely. I totally lose track when I'm at the other end of the lens.' She stood up, brushing the dust off her jeans from where she'd been lying on the jetty, and held out her hand. 'Carla.'

'Bernard.' Surely those were the biggest, brownest eyes he'd ever seen? 'Is there some kind of problem with the hull?'

'What? Oh, no!'

He could drown in that laugh.

'It's my hobby. I snap rich boys' toys, but from close-up and unusual angles, and trust me, that rail from below was too good an opportunity to miss.'

'Can I see some of your photos?'

Insurance investigators come in all shapes and sizes.

'Sure.' She pulled up a series of stunning black and white pictures, showing one wing of Rolls Royce's "Spirit of Ecstasy", a quadrant of a submarine Rolex face, part of the belt on a gleaming Maserati engine.

'You weren't kidding about close-ups. These are amazing.' He peered closer. 'What are the red streaks?'

'Ignore those, that's just my daft arty touch. Wherever I have an angle or curve, I add this silly thin red parallel line.' There it was again, that laugh. 'I call it pencilling in their eyebrows.'

'Is your gallery in London?' She was English. It made sense. But wherever she lived, this was an artist, not someone digging round fraud.

'Gallery?' she was saying. 'Good God, no. Like I said, it's a hobby. They're nowhere near good enough to exhibit.'

He spent lunch and and all the next day convincing Carla that she was wrong, to the point where, with his help (and let's face it, what else did he have to spend his money on?), she opened a small gallery three months later, barely a stone's throw from Harrods. Watching the press cluster around, and listening to the positive reviews of the critics, Bernard felt pride like he'd never felt in his life. A sense of satisfaction like nothing before.

In that moment, he knew he was in love.

And the best bit? Carla loved him.

Or rather, she loved this man who worked in the City, and as much as he wanted to come clean, what do you say? *Truth is, darling, I con councils and construction companies for a living...* There had to be a way round it, but until he found a solution, life carried on as usual.

'Don't do it!'

'Don't jump!'

Bless them, kind hearts were so predictable. But of course, Bernard did jump. Then came the diver. The knife slicing through rope. The shivering, the wheezing, the blanket, the—

'OhmyGod!' Through the haze of paramedics and the fire brigade shone the biggest, brownest eyes he'd ever seen. And they were terrified. 'I thought I'd lost you!'

'Carla? Wh-what are you doing here?'

'I followed you.' She was gabbling. Hugging him so tight, it was a wonder his ribs didn't crack. 'For God's sake, I thought you were having an affair! You kept sneaking off and—oh Bernard, why didn't I see how bad things were? I'm so sorry. Oh God, I'm so sorry. I should never have let you carry this alone!'

Struggling to breathe under her shower of kisses, the weight of lies suddenly lifted. In a quiet hotel room, over a bottle of wine, he confessed everything. From his mass-produced suicide notes to the dirty clothes that showed how little he cared, he held nothing back. Best case scenario? She'd have nothing more to do with him, and despise him for the rest of her life. It's what he deserved. Deceiving the single, most precious thing in his life ate him raw, and each day that passed he hated himself more. Worst case scenario? She'd go to the police and he'd—

'Say that again.'

'I said I don't care. I don't bloody care, can't you see that? When my husband died, I thought that car crash was the end of my life, as well. Photography became a way to escape the pain, then four years later, guess what? I met you. And today, when I thought I'd lost you—'

'Marry me.'

'Are you serious?'

'For Christ's sake, woman, just say the fuck yes.'

Carla wiped her tears and said the fuck yes.

* * *

'Don't do it!'

'Don't jump!'

Bernard shot a sideways glance to his bride, milling anxiously in the crowd. She shot him a wink. Their secret signal that the rescue services had arrived, it's safe to go over the side.

'The first time I watched you commit suicide, I was so scared I threw up,' she said.

Four jumps later, she'd managed to take control of her stomach, but was still the first to rush forward when the diver brought him up.

'I should do the next one,' she said. 'It's only fair, and I'm just as good a swimmer as you. I can hold my breath every bit as long, too.'

They'd practised together, in fact they did everything together these days, and she wouldn't let up.

'My turn next time. I insist!'

Like that day in Antibes, he spent all afternoon and all the next day talking her out of it, but once Carla had made her mind up, that was it.

'I'm done worrying, Bernard. It's only right you know how it feels, watching the person you love end it all.'

When had he ever been able to resist that laugh? 'Very well. Next time you go over the side.'

'Promise?'

'Scout's honour!'

But that was next time, this was now. Clutching his boulder, Bernard launched himself into the void, her love in those big, brown eyes washing his fears out to sea. Down he went, down, down, down, only this time the diver didn't plunge in after him straight away.

She couldn't—

Hell, no!

She couldn't have played him right from the start. Not his Carla.

He thrashed at the knot. Remembered who'd tied it. No, no, no. She wouldn't—

That business about a second gallery and a new motor yacht, they planned them together. Didn't they? The villa in St. Lucia. It was a joint decision, wasn't it? Like the ski chalet in St. Moritz, and the brand new Maserati. Just like the one her husband had died in...

No, no, she couldn't have tampered with it. Treachery to even think such a thing!

Gasping for air, he thought of the times the two of them had practised holding their breath underwater. No, no, she couldn't have been counting it out. Not his Carla. Not his lovely wife. Last week's splurge in Tiffany's was coincidence, right? Even as his lungs filled, Bernard didn't believe it could be true.

Right up to the point where... actually...y'know... it could be...

* * *

Carla made a fortune out of marriage.

Some might even say a killing.

Nights in White Satin

...never reaching the end,
letters I've written,
never meaning to send...

Carnaby Street was the usual explosion of mini-skirts, kipper ties, military surplus and bell-bottoms, with enough tie-dye and paisley to turn you blind. Union jacks were strung across like Italian mommas' washing. Hits pumped out of every psychedelic boutique. *Albatross* from Biba, *Sweet Caroline* from Take Six, bad moons rising full decibel out of Lord John. It might only stretch two hundred yards end to end, but by God, was this road shaping history. Where better for a girl to run a detective agency, than at the cutting edge of hip?

Typing up her bill for a background check on a potential book-keeper for a biscuit factory (who, despite his Beatnik beard and hippie sandals, turned out to be a pillar of integrity), Frankie wondered why it was that successful men fell into one of only two categories. Those who grew literally fat on the profits, wallowing in their wealth and lapping up the glory like a kitten at a bowl of thick, fresh Jersey cream. Versus those for whom ambition is a moving ship, always on the horizon, always out of reach, leaving them lean and spare and haunted as they chase a shifting target.

Addressing the envelope, she wondered which slot Howard Lannister fitted, but before she'd even licked the stamp, the answer pulled up, on the dot of his appointment, in six throbbing cylinders of white E-type Jag, restless written all over him. Sure as eggs, some flunky would have been tasked with buffing the red leather interior until it squeaked, and polishing the chrome wire wheels to within an inch of their lives. But that car screamed speed. That car screamed impatience. Most of all, that car screamed now. Howard Lannister was not going to be happy...

'For Christ's sake!'

Told you.

'How can they do this? Drag him off without notice for a court appearance in—where did you say?'

'Cirencester.' Such a ring of respectability, no one ever suspected it could serve as a lie. 'The instant he got the call, Mr. Mason insisted I let you know in time to cancel, but you'd already left.'

Ahem. By the time she made the call, she knew fine well Lannister was halfway to Soho.

He checked his watch against the clock on the wall 'No chance your boss will make it back today?'

''Fraid not.' How could he? He didn't exist. 'But I know Mr. Mason. He'll assign this top priority.'

One day, of course, we'll have successful women, but right now, with only Mary Quant, Betty Friedman, and Ford's striking machinists flying the feminist flag, equality seems a long way away.

Lannister stared at the handwritten note the same way the rest of us stare at an apple when we've bitten through a maggot. *'Francesca can be relied on to take full instructions.'*

'It's not my first rodeo, if that's what you're asking.' She shot him her best don't-worry smile. 'I've been with the agency from day one, Mr. Lannister. Three years, going on four.'

He searched for signs of duplicity beneath her Twiggy false eyelashes and Jean Shrimpton fringe, read the note for perhaps the fifteenth time, then finally decided he could trust both. Behind her Olivetti, Frankie crossed her fingers and hoped he hadn't picked this firm because he used the accountants next door. Especially Reg, the little bald one in the corner, who'd penned the note in exchange for a Kit-Kat and a peck on the cheek.

'Please.' She ushered him in to the back office and closed the window. (Max downstairs, smoking pot again). 'Take a seat.'

No point prompting. Lannister was the type who consider three hours' sleep a lie in, so she sat, pencil and pad poised like a good little assistant, and let him pace a groove in her carpet.

'This is extremely delicate,' he said at last.

Get away.

'I can't have word getting out.'

'Frank E. Mason is a byword for discretion.'

'I have a position to uphold.' His cheek twitched. 'Captain of industry, and all that.'

Until then, she wouldn't have called manufacturers of immersion heaters "captains of industry". But until then, she hadn't given the matter a great deal of thought. All she knew was that her client was a middle-aged, self-made man, who employed four hundred and twenty-two people in one of the ugliest factories on the Great West Road. Was this close to making his first million. And wouldn't rest until Lannister did for hot water what Kodak had done for cameras and Hoover for vacuum cleaners. Became the name that defined the noun.

Funny, though, how workaholics seemed hardwired to have unfaithful wives or runaway daughters, blackmailing mistresses or drug-taking sons. God knows, Frankie had had more than one client who'd racked up the lot, but her job was to help them, not judge them. Like Reg next door, she merely balanced the books.

'This would ruin me, if it became public—'

Don't tell me. Another rent boy under twenty-one?

'You see, I've recently come into possession of this letter.'

Few things surprised her, but that did. The letter from his inside breast pocket was yellowed and old. Old as in fifty, even a hundred years old. How was that going to sink the Admiral's fleet? Then she read it.

* * *

Halifax, 19th December, 1917

My Dearest—

 I feel I must write you again, as I do not wish you to worry about me. You will have read about the Disaster, but please know the baby and I are safe.

There is so much to tell, I hardly know where to begin, though I cannot help from wondering how you are getting on. You mentioned being assigned new duties on a different part of the ship. Perhaps you do not have the time to write, or are too tired after your strenuous shifts? I am very anxious without word from you. I check the newspapers every day, heart in mouth, since so many battleships have fallen victim to torpedo or mine, and am always weak with relief when yours is not on the list. When I see the ships that are lost I could weep, and I hope, and of course pray, you are not engaged in action in the North Sea (for that is the worst, being treacherous with mines), and that you are safe.

Now then, the big news (you will never believe it!), is that, at long last, there is nothing to stop us from being together. My! Even as I write, I feel the baby kicking inside. Surely with the same excitement that you will feel yourself upon reading my news.

I must admit, it is strange being a widow. So many of us are in the same boat, however, as a consequence of the Disaster, that I do not stand out for special sympathy or treatment, which is exactly how I like it. Darling, you will be so proud of me! How often, lying in my arms, have you told me that when opportunity knocks, it is madness not to answer the door?

*It was only when all H*ll broke loose that I knew what you meant, and I confess, I did not linger. I seized that opportunity with both hands, not an ounce of hesitation. For I am convinced that with two thousand souls dead from the explosion and four times as many wounded, it was God's will that I free ~~myself~~ us, in order that we might live together as a family. Surely He would not have put the opportunity in my path otherwise?*

You perhaps do not know the scale of the Disaster, but

some twelve thousand buildings were demolished by the blast, trees snapped in half—even iron railings bent, can you believe that? Horrific! With hundreds of fires raging at once, and the most terrible injuries (our hospitals are beleaguered and unable to cope), I knew instinctively that one more crushed skull would not raise an alarm.

Rest assured, dearest, my husband did not suffer. The pan was cast iron, and swung with such force that he did not see it coming. I would not, of course, contemplated such an act, had I not loved you from the depth of my being and carrying your dear, darling child. I rest easy, though, knowing you love me with all of your heart, and will not judge me or hold me in the wrong. You told me many times "nothing is wrong, when two hearts like ours beat as one."

Oh, how I long for this war to be over, that we may be together. I pray that the loss of the explosives in the blast has not set the war effort back too much, and shall be relieved beyond measure to hear that you are safe. I know you will write soonest, but life is dreadfully dull without news from you. To pass the time, I sing to the baby, and talk to him about you. (Yes, him! I feel certain I am carrying a boy, who will grow up tall and handsome like his papa!)

I must close now, dear, to catch the post. With fondest love, and a heart that beats with impatience until you come back to ~~me~~, us,

Your devoted girl,

Cora. x

PS: How are your chilblains? I hope, too, your chapped hands are less sore. Do, please, look after yourself, and wear the gloves that I knitted. If they are too big, you can always shrink them in hot water.

* * *

'Crikey McBlimey.' Max, landlord, friend and pot-smoking owner of the US Male downstairs, let his breath out in a whistle. 'That's what I call a family secret.'

'We all have them.'

Recent cases skittered through Frankie's head. The bookbinder's funeral, where a brother turned up, surprising everyone, since they all believed the deceased was an only child. That dentist from Holborn, looking to track down his absent father, and discovering in the process that his big sister was really his mother. The distraught couple from Richmond, desperate to find out why their daughter threw herself under the milk train.

'Cora, presumably, is Lannister's mother?'

'Was.' Frankie warmed the tea pot and swirled it round. 'She died last year, and he's only now got round to sorting out the attic.'

No fan of tea bags (they'll never catch on), she spooned PG Tips in the pot and topped up with boiling water. Not that Max admitted to drinking tea. His trademark white trousers, black shirt and Jim Morrison cut alone made him Carnaby Street personified. Throw in chiselled cheekbones, a lean frame and a penchant for illegal substances and you're looking at the poster boy for the whole damn Swingin' Sixties. Blue Nun, yes. Champagne cocktails, *bien sûr*. Even Watneys Pale Ale at a push. But PG Tips? Doesn't fit the image, babe. Which is why he regularly nipped upstairs to sneak a cuppa.

That, and other reasons.

'Odd thing to hang on to for half a century.' He leafed through the yellowing pages clipped to Frankie's receipt. 'Confession of murder, written to her lover and stressing the urgency to post, yet never does.'

'What's odder is that my grandparents live in Yorkshire.' She shot him a cockeyed grin. 'Pretty sure they'd have mentioned Halifax blowing up in 1917.'

She poured the tea. Max sipped, then lit up a Peter Stuyvesant. 'Were drugs even *around* then?'

'More likely part of a novel. The florid imagination of a bored expectant mum.'

'Yeah, how often *have* you been hired to investigate books?' He blew smoke rings in the air with practised ease. 'What does Lannister want you to do? Prove his sweet old mum wasn't a killer?'

'*Get to the bottom of it.* Those were his instructions, nothing more explicit than that. But between you, me and the gate post, I'm not expecting many happy-ever-afters when I hand over my report.'

'You think she did it.'

'I don't dig why she writes about a disaster that never happened.' Understatement of the decade. 'But I'm not getting the impression Ma Lannister missed her vocation in pulp fiction, either.'

Fingers crossed she was wrong, but there was something about the way the letter was written. If it was fiction, why that bland PS? And wouldn't you at least have the sailor writing back to his girl? Especially when she's another man's wife, pregnant with your child.

'Then fudge it.' Max stamped out his cigarette with force to make his point. 'You're in a depressing business, baby, no two ways about it. All your cases end in heartbreak.'

'And here's me thinking I'd just made a biscuit factory and a Beatnik very happy.'

'Proper cases, doll. Cheating husbands. Faithless wives. Runaways returned to abusive families, because that's the law of this bleedin' land. Everyone loses out, Frankie. Even you.'

'My fees suggest otherwise.'

'Money's got sod all to do with it. Look at me.'

Indeed. Who could miss the big, black silhouette of Elvis outside The US Male? Cling-cut crew necks and wide flair pants screamed *Buy me!* from the window, alongside frilled shirts, roll-neck sweaters and suede-fringed waistcoats. Indoors, strobe lighting flashed in time to Stevie Wonder/The Who/The Stones, but if the lights made your eyes water, it was nothing compared to the price tags.

'You won't find groovier gear anywhere in London. Georgie Best, Michael Caine, Dirk Bogarde, Status Quo.' His walls were plastered with famous faces. 'They've all messed with The US Male, but clerks and labourers buy my gear too, and so what a pair of pants sets them back a week's wages? They walk out with smiles wider than the ocean. How many of the poor sods you serve with a summons do that?'

'I'm not in the matchmaking business.'

'Put it this way, then. Can you even count the times you've rung the police, an ambulance—me for that matter—because your perfect plans went pear shaped?'

'So you think I should…what? give it couple of weeks, then report back that Mummy was the lost Jane Austen of World War One?'

'Better than have the poor bugger spend the rest of his life knowing his mother's a conniving bitch, who got away with killing the man he thought was his dad, so by the way, you're a bastard.'

She leaned against the window, staring at the spot where her captain of industry had roared off in his shiny E-type just two short hours before. The space had been taken by a Dormobile, daubed with red and green daisies and the obligatory ban-the-bomb sign on the front. Clustered beside it was a bunch of hippies in kaftans, sandals and red-tinted glasses, passing round a joint with expressions that suggested peer pressure, rather than pleasure. Frankie sighed.

'I'd not only be selling out my own integrity, but my father's with it.'

DCI Jack Mason's lifelong ambition had been to run his own detective agency when he retired, but one week shy of his fifty-second birthday, he was killed by the getaway car in some stupid diamond heist in Hatton Garden. That was three years ago. Going on four. Opening the agency was Frankie's way of honouring his memory.

'Think your old man didn't turn a blind eye in the name of peace of mind and justice?

'What I think doesn't matter, Max. By giving me instructions, Howard Lannister asked the question and—'

'I know, I know. Shouldn't ask, if you don't want to know the answer.' At which point, the King of Cool did something he rarely did. He cringed. 'You're never gonna let me forget that night, are you?'

'Not in a million.'

'It was dark,' he wailed.

'Not so dark you couldn't find her knee with your hand.'

'I was worried the poor girl might catch cold.'

'You bought her four Babychams, and told me she was hot.'

'If I'd taken my eyes off her chest and thought to make polite conversation an hour earlier, I could have saved myself a lot of grief.'

'Not to mention four Babychams.'

'I only asked where she'd gone to school.' He paused. Buried his head in his hands, before his shoulders started heaving with laughter. 'How could I know it was Eton?'

'The adams apple didn't give the game away? No, that's right. You were too busy ogling her falsies.' Frankie checked her watch. 'Listen, I should collect my Package.' The smile slipped from her face as quickly as the laughter slipped from her tone. 'It's good of you to keep taking it in, Max. But any time it becomes a drag—'

'Chill, babe.' He laid a hand on her shoulder and squeezed. 'When you first asked, I said it'd be my pleasure. Nothing's changed. Like me, the staff's happy to take turns minding it.' He grinned. 'Beats working any day.'

'It was supposed to be two, three—half a dozen times, tops. You've been baling me out for *three years.*'

He tipped his shaggy mop on one side. 'Think I hadn't noticed?'

'Going on four.'

'Then you best pop downstairs and collect your precious Package, hadn't you?' He tossed the tea cup and she just about caught it. 'Before I change my mind.'

* * *

Down those stairs, in a corner of the stock room above the US Male, the Package slept. Across a pillowcase patterned with pink rosebuds, her blonde curls splayed out like a halo, a battered teddy bear nestled in her arms.

Next to the bed, her silver go-go boots tapping to *Bringing on Back the Good Times* thumping through the floorboards, Maggie Carr, shop assistant, babysitter and Max Warren's girlfriend, leafed through *Cosmopolitan*. The one with Liz Taylor on the cover. And wondered whether being late this month meant she might—please God—finally be growing a baby of her own.

If she was pregnant, Max would have to marry her.

* * *

'Mrs. Roberts! Thanks for coming back so quickly!' The call from Frankie's contact at the British Library was a welcome relief from serving summonses, photographing cheating husbands, trying to find people who don't want to be found. 'Somehow I didn't think you'd dig up many tragedies in Halif—*WHAT?*' Frankie grabbed a pencil. 'Say that again. 6th December, 1917?'

'Just after nine in the morning.'

'Two thousand dead?'

'Nine thousand more injured, and everything within a mile-and-a-half-radius reduced to rubble. Prosperity and employment gone in a blink. Not one pane of glass in the city left unbroken.'

Hanging up, Frankie scanned her shorthand notes without realising she'd been holding her breath. As much as she'd hoped otherwise, her instinct proved right. Cora Lannister wasn't making it up.

She'd been writing from Halifax, Nova Scotia.

Not Halifax, Yorkshire.

* * *

With Europe ravaged by war, Canada was a crucial source of food, troops and ammunition, most of it funnelling through Halifax via a burgeoning network of railways and roads, with the town swelling and prospering as a result. The harbour was permanently packed with merchantmen making the Atlantic crossing, as well as British naval vessels acting as convoy for troop and supply ships.

And the one thing these vessels needed was fuel.

That fateful Thursday morning in December, a Norwegian ship, the *SS Imo*, was running late, keen to make up for lost time. Entering the Narrows at excessive speed, she met a tramp steamer sailing the wrong way. Instead of the customary port-to-port, the pilots agreed to pass starboard-to-starboard, meaning the *Imo* was facing the wrong way in the channel. Bearing down was the *SS Mont Blanc*, a French vessel bound for Bordeaux with explosives destined to shorten the war. Despite repeated warning signals, the Norwegian's pilot refused to yield, forcing *Mont Blanc* to take desperate measures to avoid a collision. Fat chance. And though both ships had stopped engines by this time and damage was slight, it was enough to flood the deck with fuel.

At that point, dockers were loading and unloading like any other day. Shift workers were head down in the surrounding factories, assembling guns and parts and cars. Doctors, nurses and orderlies were treating patients in the hospital, as usual. Shopkeepers were setting out their stalls.

And dear God, it could have stayed that way.

Had *Imo* not started up her engines, creating sparks when metal rubbed metal in a bid to disengage.

What made the tragedy worse was that hundreds—wrong, *thousands* of people flocked to watch the gigantic fire that ensued. Housewives, grocers, children on their way to school, flooded the streets, the docks, the waterfront. What a sight! They'd never seen anything like it in their lives, never would again. Come see! Come see! Come quick!

Amid the noise, the smoke, the confusion and excitement, no one heard the *Mont Blanc* captain's desperate shouts "Move back!" On the contrary. Photographers swarmed forward. Priests gathered in prayer. Citizens leaned out of their windows for a better view. Oh, such fun!

Then she blew.

You want statistics? Here's statistics. The heat of the explosion reached 10,000°F. The blast wave travelled at over 3,000 feet per second. The harbour floor was exposed when the seawater vaporised. Smoke rose 12,000 feet in the air.

Not enough? How about a half-ton anchor shank, blown two miles through the air?

Or the *Mont Blanc's* gun—rather, what was left of it, after the barrel melted off—landing four miles north?

Or the fact that nearly fifty ships were caught in the blast?

Many died instantly. Many more did not. Any building left even half-standing became a makeshift hospital for the thousands of men, women, children and babies blinded by glass, burned by fire, screaming from the pain of lost and twisted limbs, and the most terrible crush injuries you'd never hope to see.

* * *

Peeling off her false eyelashes, Frankie changed into a crisp business suit, her heart aching for the bereaved, the maimed, those left orphaned, homeless, and in shock. It ached for the poor and disadvantaged, left to fend for themselves, and especially for the black community of Africville, who received no aid, financial or otherwise, after the disaster, even though the whole world rallied to help. Ditto the native Mi'kmak tribe, virtually wiped out by a sixty-foot tidal wave, much to the satisfaction of the white settlers who'd been trying to get their hands on the land...

As Frankie turned out of her office into the psychedelic crush of Carnaby Street, it took a moment to realise that the drips on her hands were tears, and not raindrops.

* * *

'Wotcha looking for, love? Nice pair of kinky boots? These come in purple, pink and green, as well as white—'

'Peter Hollingsworth?'

His manner changed. 'You the cops?'

'Might I have a word?' If he'd misread her briefcase and navy trouser suit, who was she to burst his bubble? 'In private?'

Hell on Heels wasn't exactly the most upmarket shoe shop in the city, but Carnaby Street was still Carnaby Street, and while The Hollies kept insisting he wasn't heavy, he was their brother, cool cats of both sexes swooned over footwear in yellows, blues, silver and gold. No wonder they sold sunglasses, as well.

'If it's about that robbery, there's nuffin' to add.' The manager of this salubrious establishment led the way upstairs to a stock-cum-sitting room that reeked of Old Spice. 'Make yerself comfy. I'll put the kettle on.'

Comfy? Dream on. Frankie navigated a path through piles of precariously balanced boxes—some with lids on, some with lids off, some with not the right lids at all—to the window. How long since that last saw a lick of paint? Much less a window cleaner?

'I'd like to run through what happened last Saturday, if you don't mind.' She twisted her mouth in apology. 'Routine can be tedious.'

'Tell me about it.' Pete Hollingsworth grinned. 'Sugar?'

'No thanks.'

Unable to find anywhere to sit that wasn't covered in grime, she perched against the window sill and, while he rinsed two mugs under the cold tap, read out the statement he'd given the police involving Strawberry Junction, the boutique over the road.

'It wasn't until Barbara…' Frankie pretended to consult her notes '…Jenkins ran outside that you noticed anything wrong?'

'S'right.' Pete picked a spoon out of the dirty sink and shook it. 'I was grabbing a coffee just before closing, when I hears this godalmighty racket. I look out, and there she is, in the middle of the pavement, screaming her bleedin' head off, 'scuse my French. Her 'air's all over the place, and there's these great big 'oles in her stockin's.' He made circles with his hands to demonstrate. 'That's when I put two and two t'gevver.'

'Two and two?'

'I'd watched this scooter pull up, see?' He reached for a jar of Maxwell House and spooned it into the mugs. 'Only reason I noticed was coz it was covered wiv them things the Mods go for. Y'know? Targets? Anyway, I'd seen this bloke look round, real furtive like, then run inside. 'Alf a minute later, out he comes with two bulging carrier bags and races off, one over each arm.'

'He was wearing a paisley shirt and drainpipe denims?'

'Typical Mod gear, yeah, but the fing I remember most, and this is 'ow I picked 'im out of the line-up, was the port-wine birthmark.' Pete pointed to his cheekbone. 'Couldn't bleedin' miss it.'

Frankie accepted the coffee with a gracious smile, and set it straight on the floor. 'That squares with Miss Jenkins' account. That she was alone in the shop, one of the girls having left early, another popped out to pick up twenty Dunhills and the Evening Standard, while the third was in the bathroom upstairs at the back. Did Cassius Clay really buy shoes here?'

'Huh?'

'I saw his photo downstairs, along with the Harlem Globetrotters.' She pointed to a pair of lime green pointed cowboy boots. 'Only I can't see any of them squeezing into these.'

Pete chuckled. 'Yeah, well, the owner's got a reputation to keep up, ain't he? They stood outside the shop, though. That's when he took them snaps.'

'Ah.' Curiosity assuaged, Frankie returned to her notes. 'According to Miss Jenkins, a man subsequently identified as Kenny Roberts barged in, pushed her to the ground so hard she banged her head, then proceeded to fill two tote bags with approximately three thousand pounds in notes.' She glanced up. 'That's a lot of money.'

'Saturday's our busy day. Come the end of the afternoon, everyone's got these great 'uge piles of dosh under the counter, ready to take to the bank.'

Frankie was well aware of the phenomenon that was Carnaby Street, thanks to Max. Where else in the world would shops need vans to convey their takings to the bank on a Saturday afternoon! It was no coincidence that half the boutique owners were millionaires before thirty. Max included.

She tapped her biro against her notebook. 'Tell you what bothers me, Pete. Kenny Roberts.'

'Wot about 'im? He's well-known for robbing tills. Been in and out of prison 'alf his life.'

'Reform school, actually.'

'Whatever.' One shoulder shrugged. 'But it was 'im. No two ways about it. Me and Barbara—Miss Jenkins—both picked 'im out of a line up, and he didn't have no alibi, did he?'

'He *claims* he was outside Oxford Circus tube station. Said a man phoned him the day before about a job, they arranged to meet at four-thirty, only the caller never turned up.'

'I'm no copper, but to my mind, that's got more 'oles than a sieve. Oxford Circus is two minutes' walk away.'

'Exactly.' Frankie nodded in agreement. 'Flimsy alibis are two-a-penny, and Kenny isn't the first man to swear he's gone straight, now he's getting married.' She moved forward to look Hollingsworth square in the eye. 'But the odd thing is, Pete. I believe him.'

'I don't foller.' Pete frowned over the rim of his mug. 'You've arrested this bloke, right?'

'Kenny Roberts is helping the police with their enquiries, that's true. But you have to admit, it's highly unusual, just one salesgirl on the busiest day of the week.'

'Can only tell yer what I saw.' This time, both shoulders shrugged. 'Mod wiv a scooter goes in. Thirty seconds later, runs out with two bulging carriers. I pick him out of the line-up, coz of the mark on 'is face.'

'Without hesitation?'

'None at all.'

The perfect witness. Confident, observant and unwavering, this rare breed advanced crime-solving no end. The police loved them. The prosecution wanted to marry them and have their babies. But for defence solicitors and PIs they were a pain in the arse, and proving Kenny's innocence wouldn't be easy. For one thing, three grand's a pretty penny for a young man starting over, particularly when he has a history of robbing tills. Likewise, several kiosk owners testified to his distinctive scooter parked outside the Tube, while the birthmark only hammered nails in Kenny's coffin.

'Tell me Pete, are you and Barbara going steady?'

'You wot?'

'You've been dating since Christmas.'

'That's got nuffin' to do with it! Ask anyone, I've never met this Roberts bloke, and neither's Barbara.'

And this, thought Frankie, is the sticky bit. Kenny admitted he'd never heard of those two, either, but snatching a few quid from a till is one thing. How would he know where to find the rest of takings? Despite what Pete insisted, none of the boutique owners—and she'd questioned most of them—would dream of leaving several thousand pounds under the counter. Cash on that scale was either locked away upstairs or out the back. The important thing being, it was hidden.

Also, how could an opportunist like Kenny be sure the shop was empty?

And how often does a sneak-thief turn to violence?

'Let me tell you what happened, Pete. Barbara sends one of the Saturday girls home early, despatches another for cigarettes, then "accidentally" spills ink on the third girl's blouse, so she has to go upstairs and scrub it off.'

His lip-chewing was encouraging.

'With the place to herself, she pushes over a rack of clothes, rips her stockings, messes up her hair, then runs out screaming. Someone dials 999, the police find the till wide open, the takings gone, and her description of the robber tallies with that of an independent witness across the road.'

'Yer barking up the wrong tree. Barbara'd never pull a stunt like that.'

'Not on her own, no. But it's the sort of thing two people who can't afford to go to Woodstock on shopworkers' wages might come up with.'

Woodstock was all they'd dreamed about since the gig was announced, then what do you know? Suddenly they're two transatlantic air fares better off, according to the girl in the travel agent on the corner. Paid for, funnily enough, in cash.

'You changed your car, too.'

'We get bonuses, y'know.'

'I can see the effort you put in.' She ran her finger through the dust and left a trail. 'Now this is only supposition, Pete, but suppose someone—say, the manager of a shop like Hell on Heels—phones Kenny about a job. This would put him in the right place at the right time, and of course, that someone already knows he rides a distinctive scooter and sports an even more distinctive birthmark.'

'Yeah? How'd he know that?'

Thick as bricks, this pair. Never crossed their minds someone might check their financial activities. Or find that, what d'you know, Kenny and Barbara live just two streets apart?

'Suppose that someone goes to Oxford Circus, to note down what Kenny's wearing? Then relays this information to a girl, who just happens to be waiting at the back door of Strawberry Junction with three thousand pounds in cash?'

'I know what your game is.' Pete sneered. 'You can't make it stick with Kenny Roberts, so yer framing us instead. Well, knock yerself out, luv. Yer can't prove a bleedin' thing.'

'I don't need to. All I need to do is provide a jury with evidence of reasonable doubt, but it really doesn't matter.' Frankie snapped her briefcase shut. 'Once the police start questioning Barbara, I'm betting your goose will be cooked before it's even in the oven.' Girls like her don't go to prison. 'Deals will be cut faster than you can say fingerprint ink.'

'Jury? What jury? You said you was the cops.'

'First lesson, Pete. Always ask for identification.'

'Like this, for instance,' a rusty voice croaked, shoving a warrant card in his face.

Typical, Frankie thought. Twenty thousand officers in the Metropolitan police, at least half of them broad at the shoulder, narrow at the hip, and she gets saddled with the ugly one. OK, OK, not ugly. But a face that looked like it hit a lump of granite at 60 mph and the granite came off worse.

'Peter Michael Hollingsworth, I'm arresting you for theft, and anything you wish to say in your defence I couldn't give a toss about. Good to see you again, Mace.' Morgan Jackson, better known as the Morgue, clipped the cuffs on without breaking stride. 'How long's it been? Three years?'

'Going on four.'

And still her stupid heart kept skipping beats.

'I fort you was a customer.' Poor Pete. Genuinely didn't understand that a sting can cut both ways. 'You're the bleedin' filth.'

'D.S. Filth to you.'

'And filth's what tripped you up, Pete.' Frankie tapped the window. 'You can't see a damn thing through this glass, certainly not the detail of a birthmark.'

That, and the fact two idiots were throwing money around like there was no tomorrow. Brand new Triumph TR6, with roll-down roof and wind-up windows. Fancy clobber. Transatlantic flights.

'Does this mean I don't get to go to Woodstock?'

As though no time at all had passed, Frankie and the Morgue burst out in a simultaneous fit of laughter.

'Your father would be proud, you know that, Mace?' He shot her a tight lipped wink of approval as he bundled his prisoner down the steps. 'Suppose we celebrate working together again over a drink?'

Not bloody likely. When it came to Morgan Jackson, a drink soon runs into five, one thing leads to another—and look how that ended up three years ago. Going on four.

'Love to.' Could he still tell when she was lying?

'I'm divorced now,' he yelled up the road.

Among the throb of taxis, bikes and double-decker buses, Frankie pretended not to hear.

* * *

When Max talked about giving it two weeks then fudging the bad news, he was partly right. It took a full fortnight before the results of her searches came back, and would have taken considerably longer, had she not had a brainwave.

'Shame your boss was called to Glasgow,' Howard Lannister said, 'but I appreciate your coming in his place.'

'My pleasure.'

No run in the country is ever a hardship. Especially when your transport's a luxury E-type Jag, and it's John Constable country at that. Suffolk. Where psychedelic surrendered to the muted hues of nature, the scent of wild flowers replaced cloying marijuana, and music came from warblers, topping the charts since time immemorial.

'This must be hard for you,' she said.

And how.

Tracing the Lannisters had been simple enough. Despite the magnitude of the disaster (or perhaps because of it), meticulous records were kept, and William Albert Lannister's name was indecently easy to find. The death certificate confirmed he died from head injuries. A year later, different records tracked his widow and baby from Canada to England, settling first in Ipswich before re-locating to London, which is where Cora remained for the forty-eight years until her death, never to remarry.

But the Immersion King knew all that.

The challenge lay in tracing the man to whom his mother wrote so many letters. And who never replied to one.

'Left at the T-junction, then first right,' Frankie said, following the map with her finger.

Cora's mention of Atlantic crossings and battleships suggested her lover was part of the convoy. Being assigned different duties aboard ship suggested low rank. But Crikey McBlimey, as Max would say, thousands of men fitted that bill.

'I'm astonished you managed to traced him. There was nothing in my mother's papers even hinting at his name.'

'Second left, then straight on for two miles.' She swallowed a smile. Who needs papers? The answer—the brainwave—had been staring her in the face. Howard Neville Lannister. Odd names for a working class family. Unless, of course, Howard Neville happened to be an able seaman on the *HMS Midhurst*, making regular trips to Halifax in the course of her North Atlantic convoy career.

As though steering wheels were unimportant when taking blind bends at high speed, Lannister spiked both hands through his hair. 'You're sure this is the right man we're going to meet?'

Captain of the bowls team, captain of the darts team, tending perfect rows of peas, beans, raspberry canes and beetroots, even at the age of seventy-nine, Howard Neville had restless written all over him.

'It's the right man.'

Frankie initially assumed his father was dead. Since Cora never remarried, chances were she'd read about his death in the papers before she'd had chance to post that ill-fated confession, and let's face it. When a murderess needs a fresh start and the only thing she knows about a country is what her lover told her, who wouldn't gravitate to a place close to his memory? Except the *Midhurst* wasn't torpedoed or mined, and Howard Neville didn't die in 1918, or indeed any other time. That was the good news. The bad news was that his marriage certificate revealed he'd taken a woman named Florence to be his lawful wedded wife a full three years before hostilities broke out.

The same Florence he played bowls with on a Thursday, went to the Crown & Anchor with on a Friday, enjoyed fish and chip suppers with on a Saturday, and had shared the same terraced house with since their wedding day.

'He was happy about meeting at his allotment?'

Was Lannister kidding? Who wants to greet a son he never knew he had, in front of a wife who'd always thought him faithful?

'Nervous might be a better word.'

'He's not the only one.' Pulling to a halt beside railings that separated the road from those tidy lines of beetroots, peas and runner beans, Lannister took several deep breaths. 'All this time...Jesus...' He puffed out his cheeks, shot Frankie a wan smile, then opened the passenger door. 'Coming?'

* * *

Looking back, there were many things she didn't expect that morning, but his invitation to tag along wasn't one of them. Having made the initial approach, though, it made sense that Frankie would also make the introductions.

She'd also expected him to set off white-faced and steely jawed. And who wouldn't have last-minute doubts?

'One hundred percent *positive* this man is my father?'

'Apart from the family resemblance—' mirror bloody image '—he admits the wartime affair. and remembers your mother very clearly.'

What she omitted was Neville's dirty chuckle. The bit where he leaned forward, said *married women were always best, no strings y'know?* at which point Frankie knew exactly why he never wrote back. Bugger national security, or being too busy, too tired. The bastard didn't give a damn, and for a moment there, passing through the gate into the allotments, she almost felt sorry for Cora.

So, yes, all that tension and build-up was pretty predictable. What Frankie hadn't expected was Lannister to pick up a rock and cave Howard Senior's head in.

* * *

There are moments, we've all had them, when time literally stands still.

You can't breathe. You can't speak. You can't move.

You know what happened. You saw it. Every single detail, playing slow-motion in your head. But it's not true. It can't be. So everything remains frozen. Locked. And your head tells you that this moment must never, repeat never, end.

Because if it does, then what happened becomes real.

* * *

'I d-don't know what came over me.' Lannister spread helpless arms and lifted his eyes to the sky. 'Anyone'll tell you. My wife, my workforce, my business associates. For Christ's sakes, they'll *all* tell you. I never lose control.'

Frankie had seen death before. That is to say, she'd seen bodies. Not many, but all the same, she'd seen death. A 23-year-old teacher, who'd hanged himself for reasons she was still trying to figure out. The case last year, in which a man blew his brains out after Frankie proved he was the person responsible for embezzling funds from a children's charity. Two hippies who'd laced LSD with strychnine to prolong the trip, but in practice shortened another couple's lives.

What she'd never seen, though, was a life being taken.

The brutality of it.

The speed.

The fact you can never make it right.

Was this on her? If she'd stayed, instead of going back to the car after making the introductions, would Howard Neville still be alive? Father and son, she'd reasoned, needed some privacy. But would Lannister have picked up the rock, if she was there? Would he have smashed it down, time and time again? Who's to say, but the time she'd raced down the path, there was no saving him. The old man's brains were mingling with the raspberries he'd picked fresh from the cane just a few short minutes before.

'No one can blame me. No one in the *world* can blame me for snapping.' Lannister stared at the blood on his Savile Row suit the way you or I would view someone who'd taken the parking space we'd been queuing patiently for. 'But the second I clapped eyes on him, I was swamped. Swamped with shock, despair, the devastating sense of betrayal. All the things my mother must have felt, having given up everything to be with this man, only to find the father of her child was already married.'

Frankie forced back the nausea. Clenched her fists to stop shaking. When she spoke, her voice was perfectly level.

'You mean, the man she'd murdered her husband for?'

Lannister shot her a glance. 'Misguidedly took advice from the man she'd given her heart to,' he corrected. 'At a time when the city—her whole world—had been blown to smithereens. The same idiocy that possessed me to do the very same thing. Temporary madness, I believe, is the term. While the balance of the mind is disturbed.'

In the distance, a siren began to wail.

'The Americans have a phrase for it, don't they? Justifiable homicide?'

'You've been watching too many Hawaii-Five-O's, Mr. Lannister.' She fumbled inside the salmon pink Versace satchel bag Max had given her for Christmas. Eventually came up with a little lace hankie. Covered what was left of Howard Senior's face. 'And in case you hadn't noticed, we're not in America.'

'Crime of passion, they call it in France.' Was he even listening? 'Carried out in the heat of the moment.'

The siren was joined by another, then another.

'Except this wasn't the heat of the moment.'

'What do you mean?'

'Mr. Lannister, I was here yesterday morning.' A lovely day out, just Frankie, Max and the Package. 'I met with Mr. Neville at the exact spot we're standing now—' he'd picked her a handful of raspberries, then, too. Fleshy, sweet and juicy. Now she'd never eat raspberries again '—and trust me, that rock wasn't there. In fact, if you look round, you'll see there are no rocks in the allotment, or anywhere in this flat, fertile region. The soil simply does not own such murderous beasts.'

'Paperweights. People bring them home from the seaside, from holiday, he probably kept it in his shed.'

'He might. But isn't it odd how I was giving you directions all the way from Ipswich, but when I was distracted or forgot—' (what is it with women and maps?) '—you found your way to the back of beyond through a maze of unfamiliar, twisting lanes?'

The sirens were close now.

'What are you suggesting? I planted the rock yesterday evening?'

'In order to "seize the opportunity", the same way your mother did. You spied out the lie of the land, planted the murder weapon, then did exactly what you'd planned from the start. The only reason I'm here is because you needed a witness to this...unprecedented impulse. Oh, and to track down your father, since you genuinely didn't have a clue who he was.'

A smile twitched at the side of Lannister's face.

'Wrong. I needed a private investigator to trace him, that's true, but that could be any PI in London. What I needed from *you*, Miss Mason, was a woman's touch, and the moment I met you, I knew you'd put the right report on my desk.'

'Define right.'

'One that would accentuate the horrors of the Halifax disaster, and play on my grief-stricken emotions. One that would make me, the captain of industry who never loses control, see red at the sight of the man who wounded my mother so deeply that she could never love again, and died a lonely, broken woman.'

Was he serious? Killers never stop marrying again. More like a shortage of candidates after the War, and the harsh toll of influenza that came in its wake. Also, she suspected, there was something of the night about Cora. Something that made men back off…

'You knew there was no Frank E. Mason, just me?'

'A man does not become a successful industrialist without being thorough.'

Translation: this was a long time in the planning.

'You won't get away with it.'

'You underestimate me, Miss Mason.'

Car doors slammed. There were voices. Shouts. Boots running on gravel.

'Unfortunately for you, my next step is to sue you for inciting my emotions to the point where I snapped and killed my own father. Of course, you'll lose your licence. Shit happens. But you're an attractive young woman—'

'You honestly think you can throw me under the bus and lie your way out of murder?'

'I know I can. Oh, don't look so alarmed, Miss Mason. Like I said, you'll get married, have babies, this will soon be a bad memory—'

'Mrs.'

'Huh?'

'You keep calling me Miss, but I'm already married and I already have babies.' One, anyway. 'And it's you, I think, who underestimates me. Ah. Officer. You might want this.'

She reached into her bag and came out with a Phillips mini-cassette recording machine.

'On here you'll find everything you need to send this gentleman to prison for life.' She shot Lannister a dazzling smile. 'You were right, though.' She patted the salmon pink satchel. 'It did need a woman's touch.'

From the depths of her mind, the Moody Blues came floating up. Their big hit from a couple of years back.

Nights in white satin, never reaching the end,

Letters I've written, never meaning to send...

Cora never intended to post the letter, and risk a third party reading her homicidal confession. No, no, no. But when her lover never wrote back, she knew she was losing him. Determination, not desperation, was why she upped sticks to England. To blackmail the poor sod into marriage.

This is your son. I killed my husband for you. You have to do right by me, Howard.

Once she discovered he was married, it wasn't conscience that made her hang on to the letter. The equivalent of a hair shirt, reminding her of the wicked thing she had done. Hell no. She kept it for leverage, and the apple doesn't fall far from the tree. In fact, Frankie wouldn't mind betting Lannister knew all along. That Cora confided long ago everything except the name of her lover, and he was simply biding his time to punish the man who abandoned them both.

You don't double cross a Lannister, that was the message.

One that came over loud and disturbingly clear.

Still. At times like this—witness to murder, long way from home, still a possible suspect—when a girl's stuck in an unfamiliar police station and only allowed the one phone call, who does she ring?

Max Warren, her husband?

Or the father of her child?

'Hello? Could you put me through to the Morgue, please?'

Stage Struck

It can be a terrible strain at times, being The Great Rivorsky. You would not believe, madam, the burden it puts on a man, and I do not say this merely on account of that unfortunate incident back in Montmartre. In all honesty, who could have predicted that our volunteer from the audience had only recently been released from an institution? Indeed, it wasn't until he threw off his clothes and began braying like a donkey that I had so much as an inkling.

Of course, much of the problem lies in the word "Great". You have no *idea* of the responsibilities that are heaped upon my shoulders because of that one tiny word! And when the expectations of the audience are already raised to the highest level, you will appreciate that any failure to carry through is apt to induce missile-throwing of an accuracy that Wild Bill Hickok's Indian show would be proud of.

Not that the fault was ours, I might add. This was Salzburg, and I swear the wires for the levitation act in that little fleapit were used by Noah for winching up elephants on to the Ark and could not have seen a single sliver of grease on them since. This is the problem when travelling performances book their venues six months in advance. Theatres change hands, so you never know what you might get and in Salzburg, Pepé, our resident dwarf, was forever having to shin up those wires to release Mimi while I entertained the crowds with anecdotes of our travels and pretending that lengthy levitation was part of the act. But that night—the night the wire snapped and pinged poor Mimi into the wings—those Austrians really showed their skills in the throwing department. No doubt their dexterity is honed from generations of hurling objects across deep Alpine valleys (hams, cows, cheeses—who knows?) but all the same, six stitches in a dwarf is no laughing matter.

Flawed translation doesn't help, either. With your breeding and education, you will naturally be aware that the German for great is *grosse*. Imagine my horror, then, when we arrived in Lyon to find that some inept Frog had used my Berlin posters as the basis for his translation, stupidly putting an "a" in place of the "o" and thus urging the crowds to flock to The FAT Rivorsky. Alas, it was only under the first deluge of distressed fruit that the matter was brought to my notice, but frankly I blame the French for paying to gawp at grotesque overweight freaks. In fact, had it not been for my assistant, Inga, being hit square in the eye with an overripe greengage, I would have said it served those Lyonnaises right.

Yes, yes, of course I comforted poor little Inga. Under the circumstances, it was only natural to loosen her corset, and can I help it if she later took it upon herself to show me more than just her appreciation? She has a magnificent … constitution, does Inga, and as you know from experience, *ma chère comtesse*, I do have an eye for the ladies.

Ah, you are admiring the photograph of the dear departed, I see. Beautiful, was she not? Such hair! Such cheekbones! Such embonpoint! Dead, madam? No, no, my dear wife isn't dead, she merely departed. Somewhere between Stockholm and Vienna if I remember correctly, and my, how I miss her. My wife was the best contortionist this side of the Urals, and no woman before or after could fold herself up inside that little box you see in the corner and have me walk off stage with her tucked under my arm.

Now, then, Contessa, my deepest apologies, since we seem to have digressed, but as always with good conversation, one topic tends to roll into another, does it not? Where were we? Of course.

It started with your coming backstage to compliment me on my magic show, discussing the complexities of making elephants disappear over champagne and the dangers of catching bullets in the teeth over the caviar (and here I must both thank and compliment you on your extreme generosity). Then, if my memory serves me correctly, the talk switched to my skills as a mesmerist before moving on to my mind-reading act, sawing the lady in half, thrusting swords into the basket in which my assistant is crouching, until finally the focus turned to the somewhat unusual subject of poison.

For—and forgive me if I have this wrong, madam—but you did come here this evening to kill me, did you not?

* * *

Smelling salts! Quick, quick, someone fetch smelling salts! Not me, Pepé, you imbecile! It's *la comtesse italienne* who has swooned—but look, she's coming round. Would you mind fetching some water?

Ah, you would prefer something stronger, Contessa? I quite understand and as luck would have it, I happen to have a bottle of vodka right here in my trunk, because, in this business, one never knows when liquid fortification might come in useful and frankly, I think I will join you.

Yes, yes, thank you, Pepé, you may go now—although if you wouldn't mind closing the door as you leave, the lady and I would like a little privacy, oh and Pepé. Before you slope off to that tavern off the *Boulevard de la Reine* (and don't think I don't know about you and that strumpet from the *Comédie*—just make sure you don't get her pregnant like you did those Siamese Twins in Milan), would you mind frisking the footlights boy before he leaves?

Five nights in succession, Contessa, that boy walked out into the rain, snug inside his long flowing cape. Indeed, it wasn't until I searched for our missing rabbit that I discovered the scoundrel had been robbing me blind of my capes. Silk linings, too. Personally, I would have fired the rogue on the spot, but the theatre manager insists footlight skills are hard to find here in Marseille, and who knows? Perhaps working with gas all day affects the boy's brains.

There. A cushion under your feet will soon ease the nausea, and maybe another vodka will settle the—? My, my, it's not every day one sees countesses swigging straight from the bottle, but I think we both agree that attempted murder counts as exceptional circumstances. But rest assured, madam, your enthusiastic thirst-quenching will remain our little secret. Ah, yes. Discretion… I see from your sudden upraising of eyebrows that you thought I was about to elaborate on the subject of secrets, and so I shall, madam, so I shall. *But not yet.*

For like all good magicians, the knack comes from laying the groundwork, a principle I instil in every young person wishing to study the art of illusion. The more solid the foundations, the stronger the act—and the stronger the act, the more breath-taking the denouement. The Great Rivorsky would be merely Rivorsky, were it not for the long hours spent on detailed observation, rehearsal and training, and without the "Great", how could I have hoped to perform before the court of the Russian Tsar, give private shows to Bertie, Prince of Wales or entertain the very cream of European aristocracy?

Which, of course, brings us back to discretion. I have, as I say, rubbed shoulders with the best of them (and that Austrian archduke, Francis Ferdinand, will go far, mark my words, for I doubt we've heard the last of that gentleman). But as I was saying, it is because I have a certain rapport with the ladies—it is my life's mission to make people happy, after all—it would not be a lie to say that more than one blue-blooded filly has twiddled my moustache during the course of my tours.

I cannot deny that this was often a cause of friction between myself and the dear departed, especially since I am egalitarian when it comes to romance and do not differentiate between patrician blood and plebeian. However, it was the circus that separated me from my wife, in particular the lure of a certain lion tamer from Stamboul, but that is irrelevant.

The point is, I am well used to duchesses, countesses, princesses and the like coming backstage to compliment me on my show, and not all of them were as charming and attractive as you. (By no means). But you were the first, madam, to make overtures without the slightest twinkle in your eye. Indeed, I have seen generals draw up battle campaigns with more humour and flair, although none, I admit, with quite such dogged determination.

And only a fool would not stop to ask himself why.

* * *

At this stage, I think we need to backtrack. Perhaps, though, when you have paused with the bottle, you might allow me a snifter before I continue? After all, it is not every day a man meets his own killer…

Ah, that's better. Please don't think I didn't appreciate the champagne you brought earlier, but the thing about vodka is that it goes *smack!* to where it is needed. Straight to the point, as it were—unlike me. But then, as a magician of certain renown, I do have to be aware of my own shortcomings, just as I am aware of my strengths.

Which brings us back to the matter of observation.

I cannot (obviously!) read minds. What I can read are reactions and over the years I have trained myself to observe the tiniest changes in facial muscles, eye responses, body language and human behaviour. From this, I have honed an act in which I can "predict" all manner of things, ranging from what people have in their pockets to the words they have already written on a board I have not seen. None of the volunteers suspects that subliminal messages have already been planted both on the stage and inside their heads, and my mind-reading act both reinforces The Great Rivorsky's invincibility and serves as an interlude between what are, quite frankly, some very dangerous stunts.

I am not sure whether your eyes are glazing over due to the vodka or what you perceive to be another digression, but I merely wish to stress that, as a matter of course, I miss nothing. Everything that passes before me is absorbed, filed away in a corner of my professional mind, and some of it will be used though most of it will not, but nothing is ever discarded.

Take that scene at the train station.

Innocuous enough. As The Great Rivorsky's entourage disembarks, so a file of chained prisoners shuffles along on the adjacent platform. Even without the presence of a heavily armed guard, it was obvious that these were not petty criminals on the move, but dangerous men bound for transportation, and a dirtier, smellier, uglier bunch of fellows I have not seen in my life. Perhaps it was the effect of the steam swirling from the locomotives, but to my mind it was as though their hideous crimes formed one vast aura of menace around them, and as they shambled along, rage and bitterness etched on their faces, one realised that, if by some sudden chance they broke free from their shackles, they would happily jump the nearest individual to demand money with menaces and place no value whatsoever on human life.

Except one.

The one at the end.

He stood out, not because he was smaller or taller than the rest, or any the less ugly—there is nothing attractive about a scar bisecting a man's eye—but because of his expression. There was none of the others' surliness distorting his features, no feral glint in his eye, none of the constantly watching for opportunities for the chance to escape. Instead, there was an air of resignation about him that was lacking among the other convicts, an air of what one might almost call *calmness*.

All of this, as I say, was absorbed whilst supervising the discharging of assistants, trunks, animals and boxed scenery—tasks I frankly cannot afford to delegate, since this wouldn't be the first time poor Pepé's been left behind on a train. Being small, he snuggles into the luggage rack quite compactly and, being Spanish, it takes nothing short of an explosion to wake him. Nevertheless, as two of the guards passed us, I could not fail to catch the words "Devils Island" and I confess, madam, a cold shiver ran down my back.

Devils Island! That abomination of a penal settlement in that godforsaken corner of the Atlantic Ocean where only the most hardened of criminals is despatched and where the combination of noxious climate, brutal conditions and hard labour has claimed the lives of hundreds of prisoners over the years. With its reputation as a place from which escape is impossible, the island is aptly named. *Few who are sent to Devils Island ever return.*

But as our little group disembarked at the station, there was no time to dwell on the fate of those wretches who had condemned themselves to Hell through their own crimes. That clumsy oaf of a station porter had dropped the properties box on its head, so that swords, knives and pistols were bouncing over the platform like raindrops. With so many women and small children in the vicinity, it was imperative we gathered the weapons up fast, because The Great Rivorsky never pushes blunt swords into the basket in which his assistant is crouched, and to prove their deadliness I always slice a melon in half before we start. I repeat, some of my acts are extremely dangerous.

So there we were, in total chaos, when suddenly there was a shout.

"Look out!" a voice cried. "Look out behind you!"

Without doubt, madam, that warning saved lives. The first chain of convicts had seen the box drop and in the blink of an eye were charging down on the weapons. There is no doubt in my mind that those devils would have used the knives to hold innocent civilians hostage, killing us if their demands were not met, for these are men with nothing to lose and everything to fight for—except, of course, the salvation of their souls, where the battle is already lost.

But at the warning, I spun round and, realising immediately the danger that was unfolding, began kicking the weapons under the wheels of the train, out of harm's way. But the prisoners were gaining faster than I could scatter the blades and the guards were only beginning to shoulder their rifles. Thank the Lord, bloodshed was only averted when a judicious dwarf lunged for their collectively bound ankles, collapsing the criminal chain in one pounce.

Pepé and I made the headlines. Unfortunately for him, poor little chap, you cannot always see Pepé on account of the fact that editors tend to crop photographs to fit the available space, but the point is, The Great Rivorsky made the front page. Exactly how advantageous this was I cannot stress too strongly, although full houses and additional performances were not a foregone conclusion until the following day, when I was back in the headlines (*sans* dwarf this time) for correcting a miscarriage of justice.

You see, Contessa, the first thing I did once the convicts had been subdued was to let the captain of the guard know who was responsible for saving our lives. After all, one doesn't wish to think about what torments lay in store for the prisoner who betrayed his own kind, especially when he is isolated on a place like Devils Island! So I asked the captain if there was any way of compensating the Hungarian prisoner.

What? I didn't mention that the warning was given in Hungarian? Apologies, *madame*, but so much was happening, even in my mind as I re-lived those terrible moments, that one tends to overlook certain details in the telling. But it was purely because the shout came in my native tongue that I spun round.

Yes, yes, yes, I realise that Rivorsky is a Russian name, but this is the fault of that Harry Houdini. To use my own name would suggest I am nothing but a cheap mimic, cashing in on the world-famous escape artist and magician, when this is far from the case. Rivorsky is Great in his own right, and one day I shall be as famous as my countryman, mark my words, but to return to the railway station—

"Hungarian?" sneers the captain. "We have no Hungarians here."

"I am referring to the fellow at the end of the line," I explain patiently, because dammit, I know my own language when I hear it. "The one with the scar bisecting his left eye."

The captain of the guard smiles at me with a mix of compassion (owed to a man who has been in a life-threatening situation) and condescension (because the bumbling fool is obviously flustered). "You mean the Italian, *monsieur*. The one with the jagged scar on his right cheek."

Contessa, The Great Rivorsky is NEVER flustered.

"No," I tell him firmly. "I mean the <u>Hungarian</u> with the <u>smooth</u> scar through his <u>left</u> eye."

And to prove my point, I make him accompany me to the prisoner in question and since this is no short walk, the men having been removed from the terrified public to be contained in a small waiting room some distance from the platforms, the captain starts chatting. Telling me how incredible that such a criminal should have attracted the attention of no less than two illustrious figures in the course of a very short time.

"Why, the Countess of Perugia paid him a visit only yesterday," he prattles happily.

But I am not interested in the Countess of Perugia.

At least not then!

At that stage, I am concerned only with the man who saved my life and that of any members of the public who might have got in the way of those evil men, and how unsurprising that the prisoner is neither Italian nor has a jagged scar down his right cheek as his files record! It turns out that he is indeed of Hungarian extraction and has, as I observed, the smoothest of scars bisecting his left eye. Furthermore, his name is not that of the man listed for transportation, either. Well, well, well.

But with the ship due to sail on the next tide, there is little time (and even less inclination) for the authorities to conduct an investigation. All they are concerned about is avoiding awkward questions, and to have The Great Rivorsky hailed as the hero neatly deflects attention from their ineptitude.

Ah, but I am not The Great Rivorsky for nothing. When I see Harry Houdini handcuffed and bound, then locked in a trunk secured with steel wire and thrown in the lake, I ask myself…how? How does he bounce to the surface in fifty-nine seconds?

Thus, it is the illusionist in me that wants to know how one prisoner turns into another—although it is the man in me who wants to know why. Why one prisoner willingly takes the place of another, accepting his fate with calmness and resignation.

And the more I ponder these issues, the more my thoughts return to the mysterious Countess of Perugia. Why, I ask myself, would the Italian aristocracy travel all the way to Marseille to visit a thug in jail?

I think you had better take another swig of the vodka, *madame.*

* * *

You see, it was pure bad luck, at least from your point of view, that the exchange was a countryman of mine, although the odds are not as long as you might think. There are a good many migrant workers in Europe these days, and be they Italian, Croatian, Polish or Hungarian, they all share one common trait. They are poor. To feed their families, these men must leave their homelands for years at a time, to toil on the new railroads that are being built all over this continent. I am sure that, for a Hungarian peasant, the money you offered must have seemed like a fortune; indeed, in return for serving someone else's four year sentence, he was probably grateful to you.

One wonders when the poor wretch would have discovered that the sentence of the man whose place he was taking was three times that length? When it would dawn on him that he was to be transported, not incarcerated? And whether he had ever heard of the notorious penal settlement in French Guiana known as the Place of No Return?

To continue my tale, though, the Hungarian flees the instant he is freed, no doubt halfway to Budapest before the authorities have finished the paperwork, because he could not trust you not to come after him. But it did not take The Great Rivorsky long to work out how the beautiful and charming Countess of Perugia persuaded a gullible prison guard to unshackle the Italian with the jagged scar in a simple humanitarian gesture, that he might make what was possibly his final confession in his own language. While the guard's back was turned, the "priest" and the convict swapped places, knowing that, in the frantic scramble of transit, a scarred prisoner is a scarred prisoner and, likewise, who looks beyond holy vestments to the priest as he leaves? Especially when it is so much easier to rest one's eyes on the stunning Italian *contessa!*

You almost got away with it, until some interfering showman makes headline news with his keen eye, and what do you do? Retreat silently? Go about your normal business, in the hope that the furore will quickly die down? Those would have been the sensible options, surely. Instead, you determine to kill me.

Oh, I fully understand your anxiety.

Here you are, a rich and beautiful aristocrat with the world at your feet, finding your personal life probed by some sordid little backstreet magician—at least, I assume these were your sentiments?—where you suddenly risked having your secret exposed to the world, and don't tell me you couldn't have ridden out the danger. Even if it was proved that you substituted the prisoners, after already dropping one horrendous clanger, the authorities would be reluctant to start clapping foreign nobility in irons without a motive.

Ah, the motive…

Of all the tragedies in this sorry tale, yours is truly the most heart-rending.

I confess I cried when I began making enquiries and learned how your daughter—your only child—was abducted and killed by a monster with a jagged scar down his right cheek. Just eight years old, blonde and beautiful like her mama, butchered by a fiend, her corpse left to rot! See, I cry now when I think about that poor child, but you, Contessa… you do not. Your servants say you have not cried one tear since the day her body was carried home and you vowed to avenge her.

Vengeance, madam, is a dangerous force. It drives, but it also blinds, and, four years on, having finally tracked down the brute responsible for your daughter's death, how galling to find that he was due to be shipped to the other side of the world for the comparatively minor crime of bludgeoning and robbing a jeweller. A crime, moreover, which carries a sentence of a mere twelve years. For you, Devils Island was not punishment enough for this monster. You wished him to pay fifty—a hundred!—times over for what he did to your child and truly, I feel for you, Contessa. No woman should go through what you went through, but you became so obsessed with the notion of justice that you lost sight of its meaning.

Alas, I can only guess at the story you spun your daughter's killer when you helped him escape, although many a decent woman has fallen in love with a monster—a phenomenon that is common, if not comprehensible—and I daresay you flattered him into believing you were one of those types, convinced they are able to reform a man who is, of course, beyond redemption.

Sadly for us all, you lost your sense of perspective the day you went gunning for him and, sadder still, you lost your sense of compassion. Did you not stop to think what would happen to the prison guard who aided the escape by unshackling the prisoner? I see from your eyes that you did not expect the switch to be discovered, but you should know that he's been fired and, with his record, who will hire him now? What will happen to his family, without their breadwinner to support them?

An unforeseeable oversight, you might argue, but what about the Hungarian? At worst, he might have died on Devils Island. At best, he would have endured twelve years of Hell, returning home a broken man. Or did you think that, because you'd paid him, it was the end of the matter? That a contract is a contract is a contract…? Ah, but whether you were aware of the repercussions or not, you callously deceived two decent men, and if that wasn't enough, you set a course on cold-blooded murder.

Oh, *madame*, if only you had stopped to think! So much beauty, so much intelligence, yet so little common sense!

You compliment my stage show, but not once during your visits backstage do you mention my heroics, even though they are splashed all over the papers, and why? Because you imagined that, in raising the subject, I might suspect that the Countess of Ravenna and the Countess of Perugia were not two different women, but one and the same, and that you were on to my snoopings. Instead, you imagined that with a combination of flattery, champagne and a shapely ankle you would win my trust.

Well, I cannot deny I've been won over with less, but never, madam, without those two linchpins of life, humour and joy.

Contessa, I have played you at your own game from the start and, not wishing to sound conceited, am willing to bet that the poison of your choice is strychnine, added to that sublime vintage port destined to round off tonight's repast. As little as 0.02g would be fatal to a man of my build, with the convulsions passed off as heart failure, and no doubt when the time came for the *digestif*, you planned to have me too intoxicated with champagne, caviar and your magnificent cleavage to notice any bitterness in the taste.

So then. Having established why you wished me dead and how you planned for my murder, what should we do about it?

* * *

Oh, Contessa! My brave and beautiful countess, I am so happy—yet so sad—to see you have done the right thing.

When I left you alone in my dressing room with the port and a notepad, I knew in my heart that you were not wicked by nature; merely a loving and devoted mother whose reasoning was savaged by grief. But no longer, *madame*. No longer. And rest assured, this is the right course you have taken, although not the easiest, I admit.

The easy way was to swallow the strychnine.

Instead, you waited for me to return (never has a late night stroll been so sorrowful!) and now, my brave countess, together let us face the authorities and explain why you switched prisoners and where they can find the monster who butchered your daughter, that he might stand trial for his terrible crime.

Please. Take my arm. You are quite unsteady on your feet and not just from the vodka, but before we leave, let me just pour this port down the drain—

Oh, Contessa! The tears of grief are flowing at last. Here, take this handkerchief. No, no, I insist. It is silk, the only one of quality I have to hand, and—oh, apologies, *madame*. This is not the time, not the time at <u>all</u> for a bunch of fake flowers to pop up! But as I have lamented so many times on this tour, it can be a terrible strain, being The Great Rivorsky.

About the Author

Marilyn Todd was born in Harrow, Middlesex, but now lives with her husband on a French hilltop, surrounded by woodlands and vines.

Award winning author of 19 historical thrillers, she is also a prolific writer of short stories, most of which are crime, but which range from commercial women's fiction to comic fantasy and all points in between.

For more information and news, go to www.marilyntodd.com

www.ingramcontent.com/pod-product-compliance
Lightning Source LLC
Chambersburg PA
CBHW040822010826
48978CB00012BB/583